LOVE INSPIRED® SUSPENSE
INSPIRATIONAL ROMANCE

ISBN-13: 978-1-335-72259-1

Dangerous Amish Showdown

Copyright © 2021 by Mary Eason

All rights reserved. No part of this book may be used or reproduced in any manner whatsoever without written permission except in the case of brief quotations embodied in critical articles and reviews.

This is a work of fiction. Names, characters, places and incidents are either the product of the author's imagination or are used fictitiously. Any resemblance to actual persons, living or dead, businesses, companies, events or locales is entirely coincidental.

This edition published by arrangement with Harlequin Books S.A.

Recycling programs for this product may not exist in your area.

[F]or questions and comments about the quality of this book, please contact us [at] CustomerService@Harlequin.com.

[Lo]ve Inspired
[...] Adelaide St. West, 40th Floor
[Toro]nto, Ontario M5H 4E3, Canada
[www].Harlequin.com

[Print]ed in U.S.A.

"Open up!" a voice yelled through the locked door.

The anger in the man's tone made Willa jump. If she opened the door now, there would be no hiding the truth. They'd kill Samantha and everyone else in the house who posed a threat.

"The root cellar," Willa whispered low enough for only Mason to hear. "The door is hidden beneath the kitchen rug."

Mason nodded.

Willa quickly moved the thick rug and opened the trapdoor on the floor. She lifted the lantern from the table to give light. Golden Boy led the way down the narrow steps while she and Mason followed with little Samantha.

At the front door, the man rattled the handle. He was growing more impatient. There wouldn't be much time before he tried to break in.

She started up the stairs with Golden Boy at her feet. Before she reached the top, Mason stopped her. "These men are dangerous. If they think you have anything to do with us..." He didn't finish, but she understood the unspoken words.

"I know, but there's no other choice."

gw

Mary Alford was inspired to become a writer after reading romantic suspense greats Victoria Holt and Phyllis A. Whitney. Soon, creating characters and throwing them into dangerous situations that tested their faith came naturally for Mary. In 2012 Mary entered the speed dating contest hosted by Love Inspired Suspense and later received "the call." Writing for Love Inspired Suspense has been a dream come true for Mary.

Books by Mary Alford

Love Inspired Suspense

Forgotten Past
Rocky Mountain Pursuit
Deadly Memories
Framed for Murder
Standoff at Midnight Mountain
Grave Peril
Amish Country Kidnapping
Amish Country Murder
Covert Amish Christmas
Shielding the Amish Witness
Dangerous Amish Showdown

Visit the Author Profile page at Harlequin.com.

DANGEROUS AMISH SHOWDOWN

MARY ALFORD

LOVE INSPIRED SUS
INSPIRATIONAL ROMA

Let the words of my mouth,
and the meditation of my heart, be acceptable
in thy sight, O LORD, my strength, and my redeemer.
—*Psalms* 19:14

To the men and women
of the US Marshals Service Witness Security Program.
Thank you for risking your lives to protect those in your
care during their darkest moments. God bless you all.

ONE

Miles of pitch-black lurked outside the interior of the unmarked police vehicle. Rain peppered the hood and roof. The back-and-forth whooshing of the windshield wipers grated along US Marshal Mason Shetler's nerves. Tension wound tight in his stomach. He leaned forward and watched the road through the headlights. Relaxing wasn't an option. Somewhere out there Lucian Bartelli's people were doing everything possible to find Mason's young witness and silence her before Bartelli's trial began in less than a week.

This last move marked the third in the two months Mason and his partner, Erik Timmons, had been assigned to protect Samantha King. Somehow, Bartelli kept finding them. The coincidences were beginning to pile up and Mason didn't like where they were leading.

While Erik kept diligent watch from the passenger seat, Mason glanced briefly through the rearview mirror at the back seat where his six-year-old witness clutched the faded teddy bear tight in her arms. The last piece of her past she still had the ability to claim. Samantha stared out the window and watched the passing darkness outside the car.

His attention returned to the watery road ahead. "Are you doing okay back there, Samantha?" Mason asked the girl who had won both his and his partner's hearts from the second they'd met her. Samantha had shown more courage than a lot of the grown-ups he'd guided through the witness protection program.

"I'm doing okay, Mr. Mason."

Mason smiled at her answer. As much as he'd tried to get her to call him Mason, she never did. He'd finally gotten used to being Mr. Mason. In fact, he kind of liked it.

"Good. You let me know if you need to stop for any reason."

It broke his heart whenever he thought about what this little girl had gone through. Samantha had watched both her parents being murdered by Lucian Bartelli while she hid in a closet. During her many interviews, Samantha claimed someone else in a suit had held her mother while Lucian killed her father. Unfortunately, Samantha's description of the second man consisted of him wearing a dark suit and yelling at her mother. Mason hoped in time, after Lucian's conviction, the child would remember something more to help them arrest the second man.

Right now, Samantha remained their only witness to bring down one of the biggest weapons smugglers operating in Montana. Mason hated that so much rested on the child's tiny shoulders, but up until this point, Bartelli had been like Teflon.

Though Bartelli was currently in custody and awaiting trial in Helena, they had to be careful. None of the previous charges brought against the man had stuck because he was good at making witnesses disappear. Mason wanted to change that. For Samantha.

"How's Benny holding up?" he asked, referring to the stuffed bear in Samantha's arms.

"He's kind of sleepy, Mr. Mason, like me. But I think he's okay."

"Well, if either you or Benny want to close your eyes for a bit and get some sleep, you go right ahead."

It broke his heart that this little girl probably hadn't gotten a good night's sleep since she'd watched her parents' murder.

"We've got company." Beside him, Erik straightened his six-foot-six frame and kept his voice low enough so Samantha wouldn't hear.

His full attention focused on the side mirror. Mason discreetly glanced behind them through the rearview mirror. A set of headlights appeared in the distance.

Mason's hands tightened on the wheel while his mind went to work. At one time, he knew the area surrounding the West Kootenai Amish community better than anywhere else in the world. The remoteness of the landscape near the mountains had been the main reason he'd chosen it to keep Samantha hidden until the trial. He planned to reach out to the sheriff once they were closer to Eagle's Nest.

"It's pretty isolated here," he recalled from childhood memories. "Seems strange there'd be another traveler at this time of the night." The words barely cleared his mouth when another pair of lights topped the hill in front of them.

The digital clock on the dash registered the time. Just past two in the morning. They had been driving for hours without any sign of another vehicle. Now, two at the same time approached from opposite directions. The hairs on the back of Mason's neck stood at attention. If these were Bartelli's men, they'd somehow managed to track them down and were moving in for the kill. They'd box Mason off, force the car off the road and eliminate everyone inside, because that was Bartelli's MO. Leave no witness behind however young or innocent.

If Samantha had made even a single peep while Bartelli murdered her parents, she'd be dead already.

The ruggedness of the countryside could be unforgiving. There were few options to escape the oncoming threat.

This was bad. So bad.

"We need help. I'm calling it in." Erik reached for his cell phone while keeping his attention on the vehicle approaching straight ahead, lights on bright.

Mason's gut warned him they had a bigger problem than the trap being set before them now. How did Bartelli's people keep finding them so quickly? The last two breaches had come almost right on top of each other. Only one person knew they were heading to Eagle's Nest. His commander, Owen Harper. Mason trusted Owen completely, yet somehow Bartelli had found them again. Could someone from the marshals service be working for the gunrunner? The thought was terrifying.

"No, wait." He grabbed his partner's arm. Mason couldn't imagine someone from the marshals service taking a bribe or caving to blackmail and providing Bartelli's people with confidential information. And yet…

"Think about it for a second." He lowered his voice. "How did they find us so quickly?" He locked his gaze onto Erik's briefly, hoping his partner would pick up what he didn't want to voice aloud in front of the little girl. "We can't afford to call this into our people until we're certain."

Erik blew out a heavy sigh. "Roger that. But for the record, I sure hope you're wrong."

Mason did, too. If these were Bartelli's people, he and Erik would have to find a way to neutralize the threat they posed before the entire countryside was teeming with criminals.

He glanced to the back seat. So far, Samantha hadn't picked up on the danger steamrolling their way. Unfortunately, he wouldn't be able to keep it from her. She was smart beyond her years.

Bartelli's murder trial was scheduled to take place in exactly four days in Helena. Right now, it felt like a lifetime. Samantha had a time bomb attached to her tiny shoulders ticking off each second until the trial and it was ready to explode at any moment. If Bartelli had his way, she'd never make it to the courthouse.

Mason ran a hand over his tired eyes and tried to think beyond the danger. Childhood memories of growing up Amish here came back in a rush. The high country surrounded by the Rocky Mountains held vast wilderness areas. The Amish community of West Kootenai lay beyond those mountains.

Headlights from the car in front grew larger as it chewed up the space between them. The second vehicle appeared to take its cue and sped up, as if both drivers knew they had their target in sight.

The little girl in the back seat made a whimpering sound. "Mr. Mason, I'm scared." The fear in Samantha's tiny voice just about ripped his heart to shreds. How many more times must she be forced to go through this?

"Get down low, kiddo. Everything is going to be all right." Mason did his best to sound convincing. He hoped he hadn't just lied to this innocent child who'd been betrayed enough by the grown-ups in her life. A child needed love and security. It wasn't her fault her father had gotten mixed up with the likes of Bartelli.

"What's the plan here?" Erik asked while watching the advancing car.

Mason's mind raced with possible ways to extract them from this lethal threat. "We have to get off this road. Now." Yet the closest exit had to be more than a mile away. They didn't have that long. Which left one option— wait until the two were close. With the vehicle in front barreling down on them in their lane, if he could jerk his car off the road fast enough, the two enemy vehicles should hit head-on. *Should* being the key factor. If his plan worked, it would eliminate the threat for now. *If* it worked.

Blinded by headlights coming in both directions, Mason did his best to correctly gauge the approaching vehicles' speeds. When they were a few yards away, he yanked the steering wheel hard to the left, but not quite fast enough to avoid a blow from the car in front before it careened into the other vehicle. Samantha screamed above the noise of the two slamming into each other. Metal folded into metal. Brakes squealed.

Their car launched from the road, hitting the field to the left and spinning three hundred and sixty degrees. Mason fought with everything he had to keep from flipping over.

With the wheel clutched in a death grip as their car continued its wild spinning, Mason lost all sense of direction. The vehicle finally came to a shuddering and violent stop when the damaged engine stalled. Smoke billowed out from under the hood in waves.

"Come on," he muttered under his breath, and tried to restart the engine. The third failed attempt confirmed the truth. They wouldn't be driving out of here. He and Erik would have to take down a multitude of Bartelli's men if they stood a chance at saving Samantha's life.

Car doors slammed shut behind them.

"Get on the floor, Samantha," Erik yelled seconds before a hail of bullets blasted every inch of the vehicle. Glass shattered. The little girl screamed again and scrambled onto the floor.

Mason grabbed his weapon as the shooting lapsed. He and Erik slipped from their vehicle and ducked behind their open doors to return fire.

Several men screamed as they took bullets, but he and Erik were grossly outmanned, and they wouldn't have the upper hand for long. Another round of shots had Mason ducking low behind the door. They had to get Samantha out of the car before she took a stray bullet.

He glanced over his shoulder. The wilderness separating the highway from mountains was at their six o' clock and filled with its own set of dangers.

"Get Samantha and head to the woods behind us. I'll cover you," Mason yelled so his partner could hear him.

Erik grabbed up the little girl. Tucking her close to his body for protection, he ran toward the woods while Mason did his best to keep them safe.

His partner almost reached the safety of the trees when one of the shooters spotted him and zeroed in. Erik screamed, stumbled a couple of steps and went down quickly while still holding Samantha.

"Erik!" All sorts of dreadful outcomes played through Mason's head. His partner was hit, their witness was in jeopardy and Erik's family would be depending on Mason to keep him alive.

Desperate to reach his wounded friend, Mason moved as fast as he could while shooting over this shoulder. All around him, bullets fell like the rain coming down.

Erik struggled to get his feet underneath him.

"No—stay down!" Mason tried to warn Erik, but the noise of war drowned out his voice. He had to keep fighting to reach them, to get his partner and Samantha into the protection of the trees before the shooters took them all out.

Mason's heart drilled a frantic beat against his ears. Fear poured adrenaline through his body as he kept the disabled car between himself and the men. He bent over and he ran toward his partner. The distance seemed insurmountable with the battle raging around him. Bartelli's people weren't letting up despite his resistance. Every second they were out in the open raised the likelihood of being shot. He and Erik wouldn't have long to reach the protection of the trees.

And then what?

Samantha slowly crawled out from underneath Erik. She spotted Mason and held her arms toward him.

"Stay where you are, sweetheart." His voice must have carried above the noise because she stopped moving.

He finally reached Erik and helped him to his feet. Before he could get to Samantha, a bullet burrowed through the shoulder of his shooting arm and exited in a wealth of red-hot pain. The gun flew from Mason's hand. He lost his hold on Erik, who crumpled to the ground.

Mason scrambled for his firearm while keeping a close eye on the shooters. One man blew out two of the tires as he passed by, probably to make sure the car was completely incapacitated, taking away the marshals' only means of transportation.

He ignored the pain rolling down his arm and grabbed Erik, lifting him to his feet again. Erik's blood soaked the ground beneath where he'd gone down. Samantha was covered in it.

Mason grabbed the child's trembling hand.

"Stay in front of me." He'd use his body to shield her. "Can you walk?" he asked his partner.

Erik's full weight leaned heavily against him. "I think so." Though Erik was far from steady on his feet, he didn't have a choice. The alternative meant certain death.

Mason jerked his gaze behind them. Bartelli's men had now passed the car and were closing the space between them. Mason fired several rounds to force them back behind the car. The brief reprieve came at a price. He'd emptied his clip. He quickly reloaded.

Tightening his hold on Erik, Mason clutched Samantha's tiny hand and started walking as fast as his partner's injuries would allow.

He could feel Samantha shivering. Though it was summertime, the temperature this close to the Canadian border dipped close to freezing at night.

Moving proved excruciatingly slow. Less than a dozen feet separated them from the wilderness, but dragging an injured man while protecting little Samantha made it feel like forever before they reached the shelter of the trees.

At one time, he'd hunted in these woods with his brothers—knew every square inch of them like the back of his hand—but that was before he'd foolishly burned the life he'd once loved to ashes.

Childhood memories refused to be held captive in time. They rose from the darkness to taunt him when the past was the last thing he needed to be focused on. At times, his Amish life felt like something he'd read about in a book—someone else's childhood. But there were more moments, especially lately, when he wished he could turn back the hands of the clock.

He fought back exhaustion, and fear, and doubts that screamed he wasn't good enough or strong enough to save these blameless people.

The dense woods made it hard to see much past a few feet. They were near the mountains. If they could make it to the abandoned mines, the shafts that ran on for miles would provide a safe place to hide.

Erik's injury bled profusely. He stumbled as he fought to keep his feet beneath him. The wound needed immediate attention yet stopping right now with Bartelli's men coming after them wasn't an option.

No matter what, Mason wasn't about to let Bartelli win. Not on his watch. Not after this little girl holding his hand had given up so much of her life already to Bartelli's plot.

* * *

Golden Boy growled low and mean. The hackles on the old golden retriever's back confirmed something had the dog worried.

"What is it, boy?" Willa Lambright rose from the chair beside her *mamm*'s bedside. The dog continued to growl, its ears standing at full alert.

Before she could quiet the pooch, Golden Boy leaped to his feet, pushed the door open and left the room. He ignored Willa's calls to stay and disappeared into the house while a prickle of unease worked its way down Willa's spine.

Their homestead was miles away from the next Amish farm and close to the mountains. Her nearest neighbor was an *Englischer* who owned a cattle ranch back behind her place. Occasionally, predators such as mountain lions or bears roamed the darkened countryside near the cattle, looking for an easy meal. She might have thought nothing of Golden Boy's anxiety if it hadn't been for the shots her *mamm* heard earlier. They were the reason Willa had awoken so early in the morning.

"I'll be right back. Let me go see what has Golden Boy so worked up." Willa patted her *mamm*'s hand and put on a smile that didn't feel genuine. As she turned to leave, *Mamm* gripped her hand with a strength Willa found surprising due to her advanced illness. Huntington's disease had been slowly taking away *Mamm*'s motor skills to the point where she rarely wished to leave her bed anymore. She fatigued easily, became sad more often. It broke Willa's heart to watch her mother slowly wasting away.

"What is it?" Willa forgot all about the dog when she got a *gut* look at her mother's troubled expression.

"Be careful, *dochder*. Those shots." The alarm in *Mamm*'s voice sounded the same as when Willa had awoken an hour ago to her mother calling. *Mamm* had insisted she'd heard multiple gunshots beyond the mountain out near the highway. With her mother's advancing disease, she slept very little, yet her hearing remained strong.

Though the countryside had been silent for a while now, Willa didn't doubt her mother had heard gunshots, but who would be out so early, and on a cold and rainy morning such as this? Perhaps someone hunting out of season. It was the only explanation that came to mind.

Earlier, after her *mamm*'s claim, Willa had ventured out to the porch to investigate. A thick fog moved down from the mountains, making it almost impossible to see much beyond the front of the house, yet the silence surrounding the place had an eerie feel.

"I will be *oke*. Don't worry. I'm sure it's just an animal that's captured Golden Boy's keen sense of smell." Willa gently pulled her hand free and headed to the door. Just her and *Mamm* lived here now since Willa's *daed* passed away last year, yet she had never once felt uneasy about being so remote…until now.

Before closing the door, Willa glanced back at the woman who had been her whole world growing up.

In the advanced stages of Huntington's, at times her mother struggled to control the involuntary movements of her hands and feet, which made walking difficult. Since losing her husband, it seemed as if *Mamm* struggled to keep from giving up. Willa didn't want to think about losing her *mamm*, too.

She softly closed the door and started down the hall to the living room. Golden Boy stood near the front door with his head cocked to one side.

Willa did the same and listened. Nothing but the quiet of the peaceful countryside could be heard. Golden Boy stopped growling at least. Perhaps whatever creature lurked outside heard the dog and decided to move on.

Willa patted the dog's head as it settled

down on the rug in front of the door. "You are a *gut* watchdog." Golden Boy wagged his tail, pleased at the praise.

The animal's unusual name had come by sheer accident after *Daed* brought the abandoned puppy home. When Willa had spotted the tiny golden furball in her father's arms, she'd asked him where he'd got such a pretty golden boy. *Daed* had chuckled, but the name stuck.

The room had grown chilly with the dying fire. Overnight, the temperatures dropped drastically outside. Willa stirred the embers and added several logs. With both her and *Mamm* awake, she might as well start the morning meal before caring for the animals.

As she headed for the kitchen, Golden Boy suddenly lunged for the door and began scratching at it as if trying to get to something.

Dawn remained several hours away. She didn't relish the thought of having to face down a rogue predator in order to do her morning chores.

Willa watched the dog continue to paw at the door while growling in a low tone that meant Golden Boy was serious.

Outside, a board creaked. Something or someone stepped up on the porch. Willa grabbed the shotgun that had once belonged to her *daed* and loaded it. Growing up in this remote community, she'd learned to shoot quite young and had become deadly accurate thanks to *Daed*'s schooling. Since it had been just her and *Mamm* this past year, Willa had more than her fair share of run-ins with four-legged creatures. She didn't look forward to another one.

Grabbing the lantern from its hanging spot near the door, Willa lit it to give herself enough light to see. Her hand hovered over the door handle. A loud rap sent her jumping back. Definitely not an animal. Who would come to her home at such an hour? No possibility that came to mind was welcomed.

With her heart in her throat Willa did her best to quiet the dog without making a sound. If it was someone from the community needing help, they'd call out, yet not a peep came from the other side. The silence scared her most of all. Willa's knotted stomach warned they were up to no *gut*.

Perhaps if she kept quiet long enough, they'd give up and move on. The wish barely cleared her mind when a second pound followed by several more had her preparing for a worst-case scenario. Would she have to shoot the person if they tried to break into her home?

"It's Mason Shetler. Please open the door. I need your help."

Mason! Relief mixed with shock washed over her in waves. In an instant, the past and all the things she'd once hoped for as a *maede* forced their way up from her memories. The voice calling out to her no longer resembled that of the young man who left West Kootenai all those years ago. Yet for her, Mason would always be "that boy."

Willa exhaled deeply and jerked the door open. For the longest time she couldn't trust her eyes. Mason stood before her. Another man was slumped against him and barely conscious. Blood covered the man's shirt. Holding Mason's hand, a little girl stared up at Willa with huge, fearful eyes. She clutched a stuffed bear tight in the crook of her arm. Her face and clothes were stained with blood, as well.

"Mason?" Same handsome face. Same intense blue eyes. Yet a grown-up version stood before her when she'd been expecting the boy who used to hang out with Willa and her sister along with his *bruders*.

"What happened? Why are you here?" She forced the question out while her brain tried to make sense of what stood before her. Mason— here on her doorstep. She struggled to keep from showing her shock. Back in West Kootenai after so many years.

He'd grown several inches since he was seventeen. That lanky boy who teased her incessantly was an *Englischer*. For so long after he left, she'd hoped—prayed even—that at some point Mason would forgive his *bruder* Eli and realize he'd chosen the wrong sister to love. Thirteen years passed without that happening.

Willa grabbed the door frame and couldn't take her eyes off Mason. His dark brown hair was short and slicked back from the rain. Those piercing blue eyes that once used to twinkle with mischief now held an urgency she struggled to associate with her Mason. His face appeared drawn, and he swayed on his feet.

"I know it's early, but we need your help. Can we come inside? My partner's in bad shape." Mason glanced over his shoulder as if expecting someone to materialize through the fog.

What terrible thing had Mason become involved in? On the occasions when Willa had spoken with his *mamm* after church services, Martha mentioned her *sohn* worked for some type of law enforcement. Had he and his partner been shot in the line of duty? If so, where were the people who shot them and how did this frightened little girl fit into the nightmare?

Willa gathered in a breath and let go of her uncertainties. It didn't matter the circumstances that brought him here; *Mamm* and *Daed* had taught her to help those in need no matter the cost personally. Willa had spent most of her twenty-eight years trying to follow in their footsteps. She wouldn't turn Mason away in his time of need.

Golden Boy continued to growl his concern while the hair on his back sounded its own alarm.

"It's *oke*, boy." Willa soothed the dog with a pat, then quickly stepped aside and held the door open for them to enter. "*Jah*, please, come inside. You all must be freezing."

The little girl clung to Mason's side, watching the dog nervously.

"Samantha, it's okay." He smiled down at the child. "Golden Boy is harmless once you get to know him, and this is Willa. She's a kind person and an old friend of mine." Mason glanced at Willa. "I promise you can trust her."

Fear and distrust looked back at Willa from the *kinna*'s eyes.

Willa leaned down at Samantha's level. "I promise you're safe here, little one. Come inside and warm up by the fire. I can make you some hot chocolate," she added when the child still hesitated. "And Mason is right about Golden Boy. He's a softie. Hold out your hand like this so he can sniff it." Willa held her hand close to the dog's nose.

Samantha tentatively stuck hers out. Golden Boy gave it a couple of sniffs before he licked it and the little girl giggled. "It tickles," she said, and looked up at Mason.

"Go ahead and pet him," he told the child. Samantha stroked Golden Boy's fur and made a friend for life.

Letting go of Mason's hand, the little girl followed the dog across the threshold while Mason all but carried the injured man toward the rocker near the fire. The child didn't appear at all troubled by the sight of two injured men or the blood. Almost as if she'd been down this road before.

Golden Boy glued himself to Samantha's side, sensing the child needed his services.

"Oh, what a cute puppy!" Samantha's face lit up when Golden Boy licked her cheek. She leaned down and hugged the dog's neck.

While Golden Boy basked in the child's attention, Willa tried to pull her troubling thoughts together. She couldn't take her eyes off the wealth of bright red stains on both men's clothes. "What happened?" she asked.

Mason helped the man onto the rocker before he straightened and faced her. "We were ambushed. Erik took a bullet. I'm a US Marshal now. This is my partner, Erik, and our young witness, Samantha." He turned toward Samantha, who continued to hug Golden Boy.

"We were attacked and run off the road—" he lowered his voice "—by some bad people who are trying to silence Samantha because of something she witnessed. We managed to escape them by hiding out in the old mines, but Erik's in bad shape. I'll need to tend to his injury right away." He leveled a look her way that vanished all doubt this might be some strange misunderstanding. "Will you help us?"

Hard blue eyes bored into hers. Where had that carefree young man she'd known gone? Though she knew little about his life's work, she couldn't imagine the bad things Mason must have witnessed since leaving the Amish world behind if facing down armed men was an indication.

"Of course I'll help." She pulled herself together. "Let me get something to clean the wound and wrap it." Willa hurried to the kitchen and searched through cabinets. She gathered antibiotic cream and some gauze along with a kitchen towel. Working quickly, Willa drew water into a bowl using the battery-powered pump and returned to the living room where Mason knelt beside his partner, whose eyes were closed.

As she entered the room, a terrifying thought occurred. The shots her mother heard earlier. When Willa had been awakened earlier by her *mamm*'s worried voice, she never would have predicted this outcome. Now she understood. Somewhere out in the dark countryside were bad men trying to kill an innocent child and the two men assigned to protect her. Willa couldn't imagine a world where such horrible things existed.

"Thank you." Mason's smile lifted some of the burden from his face. She caught a glimpse of the young man he'd once been. His smile once had the power to leave her breathless and so full of hope. Back before he'd chosen her sister over Willa and her heart fractured. As painful as that time had been, *Gott* had begun preparing her for the future. If someday she developed Huntington's like her mother, she couldn't imagine forcing another person to watch her slowly die.

Mason took the bowl and towel from her. "I've got this." He nodded toward the little girl, who continued to hug Golden Boy while watching everything unfold around her. "Why don't you take Samantha into the kitchen and get her cleaned up before you have that hot chocolate." He didn't want the child to witness any more than she had already. "The blood isn't hers. She's not hurt."

Willa quickly agreed. "*Jah*, that's a *gut* idea. But once you've finished tending to your partner, let me take a look at your shoulder." She indicated his blood-soaked jacket before placing her hands on Samantha's tiny shoulders. "*Komm* with me, little one."

The child's fearful eyes darted to Mason. "I want to stay with you."

Mason came over to Samantha and knelt in front of her. "I'll be right here with Erik. Go with Willa and Golden Boy."

Tears shone in the child's eyes. Samantha's bottom lip quivered, and Mason gathered her close. "You've been so brave and I'm proud of you, but I need you to stay strong for me. Go get cleaned up and have some hot chocolate." He squeezed the little girl tight and let her go. "You're in for a treat. I remember Willa's mom making hot chocolate from when I lived here as a kid. It was delicious. I'm sure Willa's is, as well."

Mason nodded to Willa, who guided the child into the kitchen while Golden Boy kept pace.

Since her mother's illness had worsened, Golden Boy slept at the foot of *Mamm*'s bed most days and had become her constant companion. *Gott* gave dogs the ability to feel when their owners were hurting and in need of extra loving. She'd seen it enough with Golden Boy and her mother. Now the dog appeared to sense that same need in Samantha.

"Let's get you cleaned up first." Willa pulled out a chair for the young girl to sit in. "I think I still have one of my old dresses from when I was around your age. It should fit." She soaked a washcloth and handed it to Samantha. "Wash your face, sweetheart. I'll get the dress. Golden Boy, you stay with her." The animal didn't require any encouragement. He settled happily at Samantha's feet.

The child's blond ponytail bobbed as she bent down to hug Golden Boy some more. Though Willa knew little about the child, she sensed the weight of something dreadful rested on those tiny shoulders and all Willa wanted to do was take it all away. No child deserved to go through what Samantha had faced so far.

"It will be okay, Golden Boy," Samantha whispered against the dog's ear.

"I'll be right back," Willa managed, her voice thick with emotion. That poor child. Her heart ached to see the innocent hurt, but Samantha needed protection and the grown-ups around her to be strong.

Willa passed the living room where Mason

worked on his injured partner, his expression deeply concerned. From the alarming amount of blood in the bowl, Erik would need the help of the doctor who cared for the community. The sooner, the better. But if there were armed men searching the countryside, they wouldn't be able to call for help.

Willa quietly opened *Mamm*'s bedroom door and peeked her head in, hoping her mother might have fallen back asleep.

"I'm awake," *Mamm* said. Willa came inside and closed the door. "I heard voices in the house. Something's happened."

"Jah." Willa moved to her mother's bedside and did her best to explain the situation she didn't fully understand herself.

Her mother's weary eyes widened when Willa told her about Mason and his partner being shot. And the little girl with the big brown eyes who didn't deserve what she was going through.

"I must help you with the visitors. Mason is a *gut* boy and Martha's a dear friend of mine." Her mother attempted to swing her legs over the side of the bed, but they flailed wildly about beyond her control. She eventually fell back against the pillows and covered her eyes with unsteady hands. "These legs of mine," she exclaimed in a frustrated tone.

Willa squeezed her arm. "I'll handle our guests." More and more lately, *Mamm* struggled to control the involuntary movements caused by her disease. Huntington's had stolen so much from her already, including her ability to move freely and remember things that once came so easily. Each time Willa saw the struggle, it reminded her that *Mamm*'s life had become a measured one.

She fought back the familiar sense of grief and anger and tried to be strong as she pulled the quilt up over her mother's frail body. "Rest now. I'll take care of everything. If you're feeling up to it later, I'll bring Mason in for a short visit."

Mamm slowly smiled despite the tears hovering in her eyes. *"Denki, dochder,"* she murmured in a weak voice. "It will be *gut* to see him again despite the circumstances."

Willa leaned down and kissed her *mamm*'s cheek before crossing the room. With a final look, she stepped out into the hall and shut the door. She brushed tears from her eyes and prayed her *mamm* hadn't seen them. The woman she adored had always been the picture of strength throughout Willa's life. Even after learning Willa's sister, Miriam, had died in a fire deliberately set, *Mamm* had been the one to hold her family together while struggling with her disease. It was Willa's turn to be the rock for this precious woman.

She opened the door to her room next to *Mamm*'s and went over to the trunk at the foot of her bed. The dark blue dress lay on the bottom. It had been a hand-me-down from Miriam two years her senior and Willa's favorite dress as a *kinna*.

Gently lifting the dress from the trunk, Willa returned to the kitchen where little Samantha had managed to remove most of the blood from her face in between loving on Golden Boy. The clothing would be a different story. It would take a lot of scrubbing to remove those stains. It was probably best for Samantha if they weren't around to serve as a reminder of what happened. Willa would burn them in the stove and hopefully, one day in the future, Samantha would be able to free herself of the memories.

The little girl straightened as she entered the room. Willa held up the dress for her to see. "What do you think?"

Samantha's eyes brightened and she touched the fabric. "It's pretty."

"*Denki*. Let me help you change." Kneeling beside the child, Willa finished cleaning the little girl before she helped Samantha out of the soiled clothing and into the dress. "It's a *gut* fit." She sat back on her heels and admired the dress on the child. If she didn't know differently, Samantha could pass for an Amish *kinna*.

The child's attention remained on Willa, her brow wrinkled in a frown. "You talk funny."

Willa suppressed a smile and rose, straightening her dress and apron. "That's because I'm Amish. We talk and dress differently than what you are accustomed to. Now, you are dressed as an Amish girl who needs some hot chocolate."

She winked at the child and Samantha giggled. The innocent sound was a reminder this lovely little girl deserved to have more moments where she could laugh and be a child again. Not living in fear and running for her life.

Gott, please help this sweet kinna. *Protect her from men who wish to harm her.*

Willa retrieved her favorite saucepan from the cabinet near the stove. Gathering the ingredients required for the hot chocolate, she sat them on the counter. The recipe had been passed down from *Grossmammi* to Willa's mother. And now to Willa. It had always been a favorite of both hers and Miriam's.

Not a day went by when Willa didn't miss her big *schweschder*. Growing up, she and

Miriam had shared everything with each other. Willa had known about Miriam's feelings for Eli long before she'd told their parents. When Miriam married and moved away to Libby, Willa missed her deeply. They did their best to keep in touch through letters and the occasional visit. And then Miriam died.

Willa tucked the *gut* and bad memories of her sister away. They were not for this day.

Samantha watched her pour the milk she'd gotten the morning before into the pan along with cocoa and sugar. After she lit the stove, she placed the pan on one of the burners.

The child plopped down on the floor beside Golden Boy, and the dog laid his head on Samantha's lap. "Aw," she exclaimed.

Willa shook her head. Golden Boy had that effect on everyone. He was a fierce protector of both Willa and her *mamm*, but a softy at heart who loved attention. When Willa still taught at the community *skool*—back before her mother's condition worsened—Golden Boy would follow her to class from time to time, and all her students adored the animal.

She stirred the chocolate while her thoughts returned to the man in the living room. Even though she'd seen him face-to-face, Willa couldn't believe Mason Shetler was standing in her living room. Even more so under these circumstances.

Thirteen years had passed since he'd left the community. With each one, Willa believed the chances of Mason returning to West Kootenai grew smaller. She'd thought about him a lot through the years. Remembered the *gut* times they'd shared growing up. She'd often wondered about his life in the *Englischer* world. Was he happy? Had he found someone to share his future?

She shook her head. Best not to dwell too long on things that were not her concern.

While the liquid grew warm, Samantha rose and sat at the table, smoothing her tiny hands over the blue material of the garment worn by three different children.

"I like this dress very much," Samantha said when she noticed Willa watching her.

More than anything, Willa wanted to take Samantha in her arms and hug her close because she had a feeling the child needed lots of hugs. "I'm glad you like it. It's my gift to you." Willa told Samantha about it once belonging to her sister.

The child's face lit up after the story. "Oh, thank you. Mr. Mason and Mr. Erik bought me what I wore…before." She sniffed several times.

"Well, you look very pretty in your new dress." Willa tried to take the child's mind off what happened. She poured the heated liquid into a cup and sat it on the table in front of Samantha, then she pulled out the chair beside her.

Golden Boy rose and made several circles around the floor before settling at Samantha's feet with a groan. The little girl blew on the hot chocolate before tentatively taking a sip. "It's very good. My mom used to make me hot chocolate..." She stopped, took another sip, then asked, "What does *denki* mean?"

Willa smiled at the young girl curious about the world she'd been thrust into. "Your way of saying *denki* would be 'thank you.' We speak a language known as Pennsylvania Dutch."

Samantha's gaze slipped over Willa's prayer *kapp*, and she pointed to it. "Do you always wear that?"

The child's innocent questions were ones she had heard many times before. For a while, before Willa became a teacher, she'd worked as a nanny for an *Englisch* couple.

"Most times. It's called a prayer *kapp*." Samantha accepted her answer and went back to sipping her drink.

A groan sounded from the living room. Mason's wounded partner must have woken.

Two men were shot, and a frightened little girl sat at her kitchen table. What dangerous events had taken place near her peaceful community to bring back a man who'd professed he would never return to the Plain life again? And what deadly effects would his return have on her simple world?

TWO

Mason finished dressing his partner's wound, but the amount of damage left behind by the bullet alarmed him. Erik needed more help than he could give him.

"How bad is it?" The drawn expression on Erik's face told Mason the pain had become unbearable.

He knelt beside Erik's chair. Time for the truth. He wouldn't sugarcoat the situation. "It's bad. You need a doctor's attention."

Getting away from Bartelli's people had been nearly impossible with Erik hurt and Samantha scared. Somehow, Mason managed to lead them through the wilderness and to the mines without being spotted thanks to his recollection of the adventures he and his brothers had there.

They'd hid out inside a shaft. Bartelli's people came within a few feet of discovering their hiding spot at one point, and Mason overheard one of the men talking about calling for more backup to assist with the search. They wouldn't give up until they silenced Samantha.

As soon as the men cleared the mine, Mason had somehow gotten Erik and Samantha to Willa's—the closest home in the community— but with the rain falling, their muddy footprints would eventually lead Bartelli's men here.

Protecting the occupants of the house fell to him and both he and Erik were almost out of ammo. He had no way of contacting anyone with his phone still in the car and Erik's lost in the attack.

"What do you suggest we do?" The thready sound of Erik's voice scared the daylights out of Mason. Erik was one of the strongest men he knew, but he was fading.

In Amish country there would be no phones in the homes of the residents. He'd have to make it to the phone shanty near the community shops to call for help. The only problem was he didn't know who he could trust enough to call.

Contacting Owen again wasn't an option. Mason couldn't be sure his commander's phone hadn't been compromised by someone working for Bartelli.

"There's a phone near the shops in the community," Mason told Erik. "I'll call the sheriff. I don't think we can take the chance of reaching out to our people."

Erik held his gaze. "Agreed. Does anyone at the marshals service know about your Amish past?"

The implication settled around him uneasily. If someone learned about his past, they'd realize Mason might be hiding out here.

When they'd first become partners, he and Erik had shared their lives with each other. Only one other person knew the truth about Mason's past. "Owen, but I trust him." No matter what, he couldn't believe his commander would betray them.

Erik cringed and grabbed for his injured side. "I do, too, but I think we both agree that someone isn't trustworthy." He slowly leaned his head back against the rocker and closed his eyes. "I'm just going to rest for a second."

Mason rose and patted his partner's arm. "Let me see if Willa has something for the pain. I'll be right back." He thought about the innocent child in the kitchen, probably sipping her drink and playing with Willa's old dog while the world around her fell apart.

While Mason knew the basics of treating gunshot wounds, Erik's went beyond his expertise. He didn't want to think about losing his partner. He and Erik were more than work colleagues. They'd become good friends through the three and a half years they'd worked together. Erik had a wife and two kids under ten counting on Mason to keep their father alive.

He glanced down at the wounded man and realized Erik was unconscious. He felt for a pulse and found it steady. At this point, rest probably would do the most good. Hopefully, it would help him regain some of his strength.

Mason pinched the bridge of his nose and fought a losing battle with his anger. *Don't You dare take him.* It wasn't a prayer as much as an angry demand. Mason wasn't sure if he still believed in a merciful God. Where was God when he'd lost his good friend Chandler to a tragic drowning accident. When he hadn't been able to pull his friend from those icy waters. Where had the Almighty been when his argument with his brother Eli ripped so many lives apart?

Forcing the anger down proved harder than he thought. Mason studied his hands covered in blood and did his best to clean them up before slipping his jacket over the injured shoulder. Blood stained his shirt. Since the injury happened to his dominant hand, he'd be at a disadvantage in cleaning the wound himself. With everything they'd gone through—the loss of blood, the grueling hike up and down the mountain—his body had begun to slow down. A luxury he couldn't afford. Erik needed help, and Samantha had to escape this danger and make her court date. Otherwise, Bartelli would walk. If that happened, Samantha would spend the rest of her life looking over her shoulder.

He exhaled and stepped into the kitchen where Samantha had changed out of her soiled clothes, thanks to Willa. She wore a dark blue Amish dress that accentuated the child's innocence. The sight of her in the dress color of the West Kootenai community took him back in time.

Willa turned as he entered, and the past he'd left behind at seventeen hit him like a ton of bricks. She had been as much a part of the life he loved here as his *bruders*, *mamm* and *daed* and the land.

Back then, Willa had been a young girl of fifteen and a natural-born caregiver, always watching over him, her sister, his brothers… and every stray animal to venture her way. He still remembered the day her dad brought home Golden Boy. He'd found the puppy deserted near the road. Willa had taken to the dog, and Josiah loved his daughter so much he'd let her keep the animal inside the house.

That young girl he'd known in the past had

grown into a beautiful woman. Her strawberry-blond hair peeked out from underneath her prayer covering. Though her petite figure made her appear fragile, he knew differently. His mother wrote letters telling him about her courage in caring for her ailing mother while running the farm by herself.

Pretty color stained Willa's cheeks under his scrutiny. Mason shifted his attention to the little girl. Samantha would always own a piece of his heart, no matter where life took her. Like Willa, she seemed small and delicate. But she had been through some things that would break most adults.

"Mason, what's going on?" Willa asked as she came to stand in front of him. "Who shot you and your partner?"

As much as he'd hated bringing this avalanche of trouble to her door, he had, and he owed her an explanation.

"Finish your drink, Samantha," he told the child, who watched their exchange with solemn eyes.

Mason motioned Willa into the living room before answering. "I will tell you everything, but can you give me a hand with this first?" He indicated his wounded shoulder.

Her attention shifted to the bloodied shirt and her caregiving spirit went into action. She stepped closer to examine the wound while her gentle breathing fanned against his face.

Willa eased his shirt away from the wound. He couldn't take his eyes off her. Back when he'd begun his *rumspringa*, he'd only had eyes for her older sister, Miriam. He'd imagined himself in love and was convinced his brother Eli had deliberately taken Miriam from him.

He sighed. He'd been so foolish back then. If he could turn back time, how different things would be.

"Did the bullet go straight through?" Willa's green eyes latched on to his. She didn't shy away from the mess the bullet had made. It told him she'd gotten used to dealing with bad things, and that filled him with regret. He didn't want that for her, yet he knew the hardships she and her mother, Beth, faced.

He cleared his throat. "Yes. I just need you to clean it and stop the bleeding." When he swayed on his feet, Willa grabbed his uninjured arm and led him to the second rocker beside his sleeping partner. The materials he'd used to clean Erik's wound were still there.

"I will need some fresh water and another towel."

She left him. Mason closed his eyes and willed his racing thoughts to slow enough to think clearly. Like it or not, he was the only one capable of getting them out of this situation. He and Erik—and anyone else standing in Bartelli's way—would be collateral damage. Bartelli wanted Samantha dead. He'd take down Beth and Willa in the process and wouldn't think anything of it.

Doubts swam through his head. He hadn't wanted to consider the possibility of a leak in the marshals service before, but the truth stared him square in the face. How else could Bartelli's people keep finding them so quickly? The idea of someone from the same organization sworn to protect Samantha working for Bartelli chilled him to the bone.

Willa returned and placed the bowl in his lap. He winced as she cleaned the wound.

"I'm sorry. I know it hurts." She held his gaze. "I'm trying to be as gentle as possible."

"You're doing fine." Mason broke eye contact and studied the warm fire while he did his best to rebury the past. Being back here in Willa's living room once more was a shock that was hard to recover from.

"I'm sorry for coming to your house like this. I wish there'd been another option." Mason dragged in air and told her everything, including the nightmare Samantha had lived through. Watching her parents die would leave the child permanently scarred, he feared. Samantha had no family left, no one to take care of her. She'd become a ward of the state and the youngest witness Mason and Erik had ever protected. He'd do anything for her, including laying down his life to save hers.

"They want her dead, Willa. Dead. She's just a child." Disgust rose in his throat. It was present every time he thought about their tiniest witness. "Lucian Bartelli is a very dangerous man who has equally dangerous people working for him," he whispered for her ears only. "There are dozens of deaths associated with his name, and yet not a single one could be proven because Bartelli makes witnesses disappear."

He told her about their car being hit and forced from the road and about how he and Erik were shot. "Both of our phones are gone and I'm afraid we won't have much time before this place is crawling with Bartelli's men." A fear he hated to see entered her eyes. "If I can borrow your buggy long enough to go to the phone shanty near the community shops, I believe the sheriff over in Eagle's Nest can help get us out of here. I can save my partner and keep Samantha safe."

Her face softened in a familiar look of sympathy. "Of course you can. But you should use the enclosed buggy. It will allow you to stay out of sight mostly."

"Thank you." He clasped her hands. "I promise we won't stay long."

Before she had the chance to answer, a noise at the front of the house grabbed their attention. Willa whirled toward it. The porch groaned under the weight of someone's footsteps.

Too late, tore through his head.

Mason held his finger to his lips and hurried to the kitchen with Willa. He grabbed Samantha. The dog had risen and sniffed the air around him. Someone pounded on the door. Without a doubt, Bartelli's men had tracked their footprints to Willa's home. If forced into a shootout with Erik severely injured and Mason's hurt shoulder, he wasn't sure he could protect the lives at stake in this simple Amish home.

"Open up!" a voice Willa didn't recognize yelled through the locked door. The anger in the man's tone made her jump. If she opened the door now, there would be no hiding the truth.

Golden Boy barked aggressively and charged for the door. Willa grabbed the animal's collar and tried her best to quiet him as the man continued to demand entrance to the house. If she didn't open the door soon, they'd break it down. After the things Mason had told her about the man they worked for, she knew they'd kill Samantha and everyone else in the house who posed a threat.

"The root cellar," Willa whispered low enough for only Mason to hear. "The door is hidden beneath the kitchen rug. If you didn't know it was there, you wouldn't expect there to be another room below the kitchen."

Mason nodded. "Stay here, Samantha." He sat the little girl on her feet, then turned to Willa. "Help me with Erik."

Golden Boy trotted over in a protective gesture and licked the child's hand. Willa returned to the living room with Mason and grabbed one of Erik's arms while Mason hoisted his partner to his feet. Erik gave a weak groan. Willa stopped midstride and stared at Mason. She prayed the man outside hadn't heard.

"We must hurry," she whispered.

They carried the unconscious man into the kitchen where Samantha watched them with wide, fearful eyes.

Willa quickly moved the thick rug her *mamm* had knit and opened the trapdoor on the floor. She lifted the lantern from the table to give light. Golden Boy led the way down the narrow steps while she and Mason managed to get Erik safely to the root cellar.

At the front door, the man rattled the handle. He was growing more impatient. There wouldn't be much time before he tried to break in.

She started up the stairs with Golden Boy at her feet. Before she reached the top, Mason stopped her. "These men are dangerous. If they think you have anything to do with us…" He didn't finish, but she understood the unspoken words.

"I know, but there's no other choice." With a final look into Mason's worried eyes, Willa hurried up the stairs and closed the trapdoor as quietly as possible. She replaced the rug and went to the living room. The bowl and supplies used to bandage Mason and Erik's injuries were still in the living room. Both men's bloodied jackets were lying on the floor nearby.

"Open up. Last chance or I'm breaking down the door."

Golden Boy growled several times, then barked his displeasure.

"I'm coming." Willa quickly gathered the jackets and other items and shoved them into the closest cabinet before pouring the water down the sink. Spotting Samantha's soiled clothing, she shoved them into the same cabinet.

Willa surveyed the kitchen carefully. Samantha's cup still sat on the table. She carried it to the sink and rinsed it out. Once she was satisfied all the evidence was gone from the kitchen and living area, she grabbed the shotgun and took up the lantern. No matter what she'd face, *Gott* would protect her, and Golden Boy would fight to the death to save her life.

With a final glance around the living room, Willa unlocked the door and opened it. Several men stood on the porch, and all seemed surprised by her Amish appearance.

The man closest to the door stepped into her personal space. "Where are they?" he demanded in a voice that sent chills down her spine. His angry gaze bored into hers.

Golden Boy, sensing a threat from the man, barred his teeth and snarled fiercely. The man's attention jerked to the animal. "Restrain your dog or I'll do it for you."

Willa grabbed Golden Boy's collar. "He's just protecting me." Though she was quaking all over, Willa did her best to keep her fears to herself. "Why are you here? I don't know who you're talking about. It's just me and my mother living here."

"Don't give me that." The lead man shoved

her aside and came in along with his men. "There are footprints everywhere outside your home. All over the porch." He waved a hand toward the open door and stepped to within a few inches of Willa. "They're here. Bring them out and you and your mother won't get hurt."

Keeping Golden Boy secured became a difficult task. The dog lunged for the man who had shoved her.

"Heel, Golden Boy," she said when the man pointed a gun at the dog. Willa tried not to show a reaction to his threat or aggressive behavior toward her dog. "I told you, there's no one here but me and my mother, and she isn't well." She lifted her chin and stood her ground when the stranger clenched his fists.

"Search the place," he ordered without breaking eye contact with Willa.

She couldn't believe his boldness. "Stop. You have no right to do such a thing. Who are you?"

The men ignored her entirely and responded quickly. They spread out through the small home. One man headed for her mother's room.

"That's not your concern. We have our orders and we're going to follow them. You'd better not be lying to me."

All she could think about was how terrified her mother would be when a stranger entered her room. She started past the man to be with her mother, but he grabbed her arm in a painful grip. "No, you don't. You're staying with me. We can't have you trying to warn them, now can we?"

Golden Boy lunged again. It took all the strength Willa could muster to hold the animal back. She didn't want this man to shoot her dog.

Helpless to do anything, Willa watched her mother's bedroom door anxiously. What was happening? Why would it take so long to search *Mamm*'s small bedroom? *Please don't let that man hurt her.*

Willa tried to pull free of the man's painful grip, but he forced her along with him to the kitchen. Somehow, she held on to Golden Boy's collar even as the man relentlessly dragged her against her will.

Once they were in the kitchen, he let her go and moved to the middle of the room, standing right on the rug covering the door to the root cellar. A corner of the rug was turned up. She held her breath. What would happen if he noticed it?

The man went to the sink and glanced out the window briefly, then down to the sink. Had she gotten rid of all the bloodstains? Her heart accelerated when he rested his hands on either side of it. The darkness outside the window reflected an angry scowl on his face.

He whirled toward Willa and pinned her with his glare. Willa fought against looking at the turned-up rug.

"What's in the barn?" he snapped. She shrank back and tried to find her voice over the fear pumping through her body.

"Nothing. Our family buggies and the animals that sustain the farm. We're Amish. We're peaceful people and not part of whatever illegal activity you are pursuing. Please leave us alone."

He snorted his disbelief. "Everyone is capable of violence given the opportunity. Even you, Amish lady." He took a threatening step closer and the dog pulled against Willa's restraint.

The man's eyes narrowed. He kept a close watch on Golden Boy. Rage appeared to be boiling inside him, and Willa feared the situation would turn volatile at any moment.

Please, Gott, *protect us all.*

The other men came into the room. "There's no one here but an old lady, and she's sleeping," one said. "We looked everywhere."

The leader continued to stare Willa down with a seething look that appeared to be his normal expression. After a long terrifying moment, he blew out a sigh. "Perhaps we were wrong. Maybe they moved on. Still, you won't mind if we search the barn in case they are hiding in there." It wasn't a question, and he didn't wait for an answer. He motioned to the three men who headed out the still-open front door.

Once they'd left, the leader stepped closer to Willa. "If you know where they are, and you aren't telling us…" He didn't finish. The unspoken threat stood between them as the man started past her. She held her breath when he stopped suddenly after spotting the folded-up corner of the rug. Would he guess there was another room beneath the house?

He kept his attention on her face while Willa tried to hold on to a blank expression. Her heart ticked off each passing second before he kicked the rug corner over and followed his men out into the rainy darkness.

Relief rushed through Willa's limbs. She bent over and sucked in several cleansing gulps before straightening. For the longest time, she held on to the dog's collar and couldn't stop shaking. The cold of the early morning rushed into the room, snapping her into action. The door remained open and unlocked. She and her mother were vulnerable. What if they decided to come back and question her again?

A shiver of apprehension slipped between her shoulder blades.

With her hand still holding Golden Boy's collar to keep her protector from charging after them, Willa moved to the living room and stepped out the door in time to see flashlights bouncing past the barn that was off to the right side of the house. They were heading for the woods beyond it. They'd finished searching the structure and were moving on, but she didn't believe she'd seen the last of them, and that terrified her.

Her family home would be the closest to the old mines where Mason had said they'd been and the logical place where someone hiding inside the mines might go. The porch was covered with footprints from the men as well as from Mason, Erik and Samantha. The man had mentioned seeing the prints, so would he really write her home off so easily? She wondered if they would fall back into the woods and watch her place or search the rest of the properties on this side of the mountains.

There were several *Englischer* ranches around. Ethan Connors's ranch lay behind her homestead. Their neighbor was a kind man who checked in on her *mamm* from time to time.

Willa shivered as she thought about the

anger she'd witnessed in the leader's eyes. She didn't want another run-in with him or his men, but she didn't want him to harm her neighbors, either.

She hurried back inside the house and clicked the lock into place. Willa couldn't imagine how scared her *mamm* must be after having a strange man enter her room, much less searching it. Despite what the man had said about her being asleep, Willa knew her mother would have been aware of someone in her room.

With Golden Boy at her side, Willa opened her mother's door. The dog trotted inside and over to the bed where he licked *Mamm*'s hand.

"Did they leave?" *Mamm* opened her eyes.

"*Jah*, they are gone. Did they hurt you?"

"*Nay.* I pretended to be sleeping, but they still nosed around the room. Looked under the bed. They opened my drawers," she said with outrage. "Who were they?"

Her mother's courage made her proud. "I'm sorry you had to go through that. They came here looking for Mason and the little girl he and his partner are protecting. I hid them in the root cellar when the men arrived. I should go check on them, but I'll be back to talk to you soon."

Mamm lifted her shaky hands in a shooing motion. "Go. I'll be fine."

Willa clutched her mother's hands and kissed her forehead. "Stay here, Golden Boy." The animal settled in at the foot of the bed yet remained alert.

She stepped out into the hall and closed the door behind her while tamping down her anger at those dangerous men. Mason had said they were ruthless. Now she'd seen it firsthand. How could they harass a woman so ill?

In the kitchen, her attention fell on the rug. She believed it was by *Gott*'s own intervention that the leader hadn't discovered the entrance to the cellar.

Willa grabbed the lantern from the kitchen table and tossed back the rug. She opened the trapdoor and started down the steps. Mason knelt beside his partner, who sat up now, fully alert. Samantha had sandwiched herself between her two protectors. The fearful look on the child's face was a reminder of what she'd gone through. And the nightmare situation was far from over.

"Have they left the property?" Mason's worried eyes held hers.

Willa knelt beside him. "I'm not sure. I saw their flashlights past the barn. They searched the house and barn. I think they believed me when I told them it was just me and *Mamm*."

"I hope you're right." But Mason's tone held doubt. He faced his partner. "Let's get you back upstairs by the fire. You're shaking."

Erik rose under his own accord and managed to make it up the steps with Mason's help. The effort quickly took its toll. When he reached the living room, Erik sank back into the rocker clutching his side. Willa brought over a blanket from the chest near the sofa and covered Erik with it while Mason added more wood to the stove.

"I have something for the pain." She went to the kitchen and brought out the pain medicine her mother used occasionally. She handed him two pills and some water.

Erik swallowed the medicine and handed her back the water. "Thank you." He leaned his head against the back of the chair once more.

Soon, the fire blazed warm again. Erik closed his eyes, his breathing labored. The bullet must have done a lot of damage to be able to take down a fit man like Erik. She worried if the wound was infected. If that happened, Erik could die.

Despite the heat from the fire, Willa couldn't stop shaking, either. Not from the cold as much from the danger that had showed up at her door. And she feared that was just the jumping-off point for something much worse.

THREE

They'd managed to escape Bartelli's men for now, but he feared it had only bought them a short reprieve. Soon, the entire area would be saturated with Bartelli's soldiers. When that happened, they'd comb every square inch of the community, searching house to house until they found what they were looking for. In a community this small, staying hidden for long would be impossible. Sooner or later, he had to make a move. He just didn't want it to be the wrong one.

If he could borrow a set of Willa's dad's clothing to use as a disguise, perhaps he could fool the men into believing he was an Amish man should he stumble upon them before he reached the phone shanty.

"Do you still have some of your dad's clothing?" Mason told her his plan and she didn't hesitate.

"*Jah*, I do. I'll get them for you, but what

about your injury? Driving a buggy in the fog and rain is hard enough. The mare will be spooked after all the strange men in her home."

Mason worried more about his partner than controlling the animal. "I'll be fine." He lowered his voice. "I need you here to protect Samantha. Erik's in no shape to fight off Bartelli's people should they return and realize you hid us." But leaving Willa alone would put her in danger. She wasn't equipped to handle so many dangerous men by herself. He ran a hand across the back of his neck. Without help, Erik might not make it. He faced a no-win situation and hoped he made the right call.

Erik moaned, drawing Mason's attention. The injured man sat up straighter and opened his eyes. "Where's Samantha?" he asked when he became aware of his surroundings.

Mason moved closer and squeezed his partner's arm. "She's safe, brother. Right over there." He pointed to the sofa nearby where Samantha held Benny close and watched her protectors with a worried frown.

Erik nodded and appeared to struggle for air. "What's the plan? Bartelli's men are still out there somewhere." He looked up at Mason with glazed eyes.

Mason hesitated. As a marshal sworn to protect Samantha, Erik would wish to fight Bartelli with everything he had, but the best thing for him was rest.

"I don't have a choice. I'm going to the phone shanty. I'll change into some Amish clothing and take Willa's family buggy."

Erik obviously had his doubts. "If what we suspect is true about a dirty marshal, I sure hope you can trust the sheriff. I don't know anything about him."

But Mason did. "He's an honorable man. He'll do the right thing."

But before he left, he needed to see Willa's mother. Beth hadn't been up and about since they'd arrived at her house.

He shifted toward Willa. "Where's your mother?" In the letters his mother had written to him through the years, she'd mentioned how seriously ill Beth had become.

"In her room," Willa said quietly, a sad look replacing her worry for him. "She isn't well. *Mamm* rarely leaves her room anymore."

He hated hearing this about Beth. She'd been like a second mother to him and his brothers since her family moved to West Kootenai from St. Ignatius. "My mother catches me up on the community news from time to time. She mentioned Beth's health issues. I'm so sorry."

Willa swallowed several times. *"Denki."* Her voice was little more than a whisper. "I wish I could erase this horrible disease from her body, but I can't." She lifted her palms up. Less than a year earlier, Willa had buried her father. Now her mother's illness grew worse. Mason couldn't imagine the pain she'd gone through watching the once vibrant Beth slowly wasting away.

"I miss the woman she was before. So full of life." The tears in Willa's eyes made him want to take her in his arms and tell her everything would be fine. To grieve with her for the woman who had always been so lovely to him and his family. But he couldn't because everything would not. When he'd learned about Beth's diagnosis it had been devastating because the disease had no cure. It was virtually a death sentence.

"She has her *gut* days, but mostly…" Willa stopped, pulled in a breath. "Mostly, she is bedridden."

Mason couldn't imagine how difficult Beth's life had become. Before Josiah had passed, Beth had lost her daughter Miriam a little more than two years earlier. The family had suffered more than its share of tragedy.

"I heard about Josiah. I'm so sorry." He inhaled and took her hands in his. "And about Miriam," he added quietly. "I know how close you two were." Still today, the news of Miriam's tragic passing was hard to comprehend. How could someone wish to hurt such a kind woman. She'd died in a fire deemed arson. The man responsible for ending her life now served a prison sentence.

When the news of Miriam's death caught up with him, Mason wasn't sure what he'd feel. But his first thought was for his brother. How hard it must have been for Eli to lose his wife in such a terrible way.

Miriam's passing had brought up all the guilt Mason had lived with for years. Imagining himself in love with Willa's older sister, he'd been so certain she would return his affections. When she'd chosen his brother, his world had fallen apart. He'd blamed Eli for taking Miriam from him—told him he no longer wanted to be his brother—and had severed all contact with Eli by leaving West Kootenai and the life he loved behind. He'd been too young to realize his behavior had much deeper roots. And his teenage crush hadn't lasted much longer than the time it took for him to leave his family and the faith.

Mason had eventually realized it wasn't Miriam's rejection that drove him away. It was losing his friend Chandler. He hadn't dealt with the loss and had projected his feelings of anger onto his brother. Stubborn pride had kept him from returning. The passing time made him question if he could ever possibly hope to fix the damage he'd done.

"*Denki*," Willa murmured softly, drawing his attention back to her pretty face, which revealed so much pain. "I miss Miriam." She shrugged helplessly and pulled her hands from his. "At times, I still can't believe she's gone." Willa had witnessed part of the ugly argument between him and Eli, and for that he was sorry.

"*Mamm* knows some about what's happening now," she told him. "I explained what I could, but the rest of the story should come from you."

She spoke the truth. Beth deserved to hear the full story and he would tell it to her, but he had to be quick.

Mason turned back to his partner. "I'll be right back." Erik didn't open his eyes and Mason studied his wounded friend. Some of Erik's color had returned, though he didn't believe it would last. He'd seen the damage the bullet had done, and it hadn't exited. It remained inside Erik's body, festering.

"Let's go speak with your mother," Mason told Willa. He'd taken but a few steps when Samantha jumped from the sofa with Benny held tight against her chest and ran after him. He held out his hand. "Come and meet a good friend of mine." She clung to his side as if terrified of being left behind. Mason struggled to let go of the anger he felt toward Samantha's father. How had he let himself get involved with someone like Bartelli?

With Samantha's tiny hand tucked in his, Mason silently vowed he'd bring Bartelli down. No matter the cost, this sweet little girl deserved to have a happy life.

He followed Willa down the hall to the last room on the right.

She stuck her head into the room. "She's awake." Willa went inside and held the door open for them. "I've brought you visitors."

Samantha clutched his hand tighter as they stepped into the darkened room. The dog near Beth's bed jumped to his feet in a defensive gesture.

"It's *oke*, Golden Boy. It's our friends," Willa told the animal, who appeared rattled from his earlier encounter with Bartelli's people. After a second or two, the dog accepted her answer and reclaimed his spot.

Mason's eyes slowly adjusted to the lack of light. Seeing Beth confined to the bed made it hard not to show a reaction. In his mind, Beth remained captured in a time capsule from thirteen years earlier. Smiling and full of life. Always there for her family and her community. She'd accepted Mason and his brothers into her family. Feeding them. Putting them to work. Beth and Josiah invited the brothers in for their Bible readings. He could still feel Beth swatting at his hand when she'd caught him tugging on Miriam's prayer *kapp* instead of listening to the Word.

Though he swallowed several times, the lump in his throat wouldn't go away as he faced the fragile woman lying in the bed. She seemed a shadow of the person he remembered from his youth. The ravages of the disease were there in the weight loss, her drawn features and the uncontrolled shaking of her limbs.

A rush of anger washed over him. His free hand balled into a fist at his side. How unfair for Beth to be stricken with such a merciless disease. She didn't deserve this death sentence. He wanted to scream at God for allowing this to happen. Hadn't Beth and Willa suffered enough?

When Beth got a good look at him, her face creased into a smile. "Mason," she exclaimed, and held out her trembling arms like she had so many times in his youth. Mason briefly released Samantha's hand to lean down and hug her frail body. He worried even the gentlest of touches might crush her. Tears he hadn't experienced in a long time were close, yet he refused to set them free. He wouldn't be anything but strong for this fearless woman trapped in a body betraying her.

"Beth, it's good to see you again," he managed, though his voice had a catch in it. "I've missed you." The admission came out almost of its own accord, yet he didn't regret speaking the truth. He'd thought a lot about Beth, missed her quirky sense of humor.

She squeezed him closer and he struggled to keep from wincing in pain. After everything Beth was going through, a little thing like being shot seemed somewhat trivial right now.

When he would have moved away, Beth grasped his hand and held it in a surprisingly strong grip. "You've been missed, as well. By me, my *dochder*, your *mamm* and your *bruders*." Beth always spoke the truth. Still he found it difficult to believe his brothers would miss him after the problems he'd caused.

"And who is this with you?"

Mason turned to the child who had stuck to his side like Velcro.

"This is Samantha. Samantha, this is Beth, Willa's mother. I practically grew up with Willa and her sister. Beth here is one of the nicest people you will ever meet. But don't believe everything she tells you about me." He winked at the child.

Beth chuckled. Her gaze swept over the child clothed in her daughter's old dress. "Well, it's nice to meet you, Samantha. And who do you have there?" She pointed to the bear peeking out from the crook of Samantha's arm.

Samantha slowly held up the bear for Beth to see. If anyone could gain the child's trust, it was Beth. She had a gentle way about her that made everyone feel at ease.

"That's an awfully fine-looking bear indeed. What's his name?"

Samantha looked to Mason, who nodded.

"This is Benny," Samantha's high voice announced proudly. She held the bear closer for Beth to observe.

Beth clasped the stuffed animal's arm and pretended to shake its hand. "Nice to meet you, Benny. Welcome to my home." Beth's gaze returned to Mason. "Willa tells me you've been hurt." She pointed to his shoulder.

"It's nothing." He dismissed her concern and did his best to explain the complicated situation they now faced, keeping in mind the child standing close.

Beth shook her head. "Those people are up to no *gut*. One of them searched my room. I didn't know what he might do."

Mason regretted putting Beth through such an ordeal. "I'm terribly sorry. I realize we are putting you and Willa in jeopardy, but I promise we won't stay long. Willa has agreed to let me use the buggy to ride to the phone. Once the sheriff arrives, we'll get out of your hair."

Beth squeezed his hand with a strength that reminded him of the woman he'd known at seventeen. "*Nay*, you're welcome to stay here as long as you need, Mason Shetler. You're like one of my own. Always have been. Hopefully, those bad men will move on."

He didn't feel deserving of her kindness and struggled to keep his emotions in check. Being back here, seeing this gentle woman and remembering all the good times he'd spent with her, Josiah, Willa and Miriam, made it hard not to get a little choked up. While he didn't believe Bartelli's people would leave the area so easily, he kept his doubts to himself.

"Thank you, Beth, but these men are extremely dangerous. They work for a man who floods the country with weapons to sell to street gangs. And that's just part of Bartelli's criminal empire. Our being here is putting you and Willa in danger. That's not what I want. As soon as we're able, we'll move on."

"West Kootenai will always be your home, Mason. No matter how far you roam, or what trouble is brewing in that head of yours, this is home," she stressed almost as if she were in his head. A smile creased Beth's face, reminding him of the woman from his childhood. She looked Mason up and down. "You finally filled out. You were always such a skinny boy."

Despite his concerns, Mason chuckled. "Yes, even though you constantly fed me." His heart overflowed with memories. "You always were good to me and my brothers." He didn't want to lose her to this disease. There'd been too much death already—his friend Chandler, his grandfather, his father, Josiah…and Miriam. He didn't want to lose another piece of his heart.

"That's because you are *gut* boys. All of you." Green eyes, so much like both of her daughters', held his. Beth was being kind. Mason still remembered the difficult kid he'd been growing up. He'd been headstrong, determined, impulsive and so sure he knew everything. At seventeen, he thought he had life all worked out. He and his brother Fletcher, along with Chandler, would start a hunting guide business to help other hunters navigate the mountains for game. And if he could talk his brother and Chandler into it, they'd assist the sheriff with the search-and-rescue missions that took place each year in the high country.

After all, the brothers knew the mountains and the dangers there better than anyone.

But then Chandler died, and everything changed. His world was sent into a tailspin and he'd latched on to something that didn't exist.

"You are a strong man, Mason, but you must be careful." Beth's warning pulled him from the past. "You have many people depending on you."

He looked to the child, who had clasped his hand again, and he understood fully the stakes. The injustice that had been dealt to Samantha was more than any human being should have to endure, and the weight resting on Mason's shoulders was staggering.

"*Gott* will help you carry the burden."

Shocked, Mason stared at the woman who still could read him like a book. She knew whenever he'd done something he shouldn't. Or kept his grief bottled up. Beth had been the one to warn him about not letting his feelings out. She'd told him if he didn't, the hurt would find its own path of freedom, much like a river. And she'd been right.

Her eyes fluttered closed. Beth heaved a sigh as if the short visit had taken its toll.

"We should let you get some rest." He didn't want to tire Beth out.

He turned to leave, but a whisper stopped

him. "It's nice to have a *kinna* in the house again. It's been a long time since my girls were so young."

Mason struggled to keep from losing it. This strong and Godly woman had lost so much. He squeezed her arm. "I'm sorry about Miriam and Josiah. They were both good people." His sentiments felt inadequate.

A hint of a smile touched Beth's lips. "They were indeed. *Denki*, Mason."

Samantha pulled her hand free of his and inched over to Beth's bed. "Are you getting sleepy?" The child leaned her elbows on the bed with the bear wagging in her hand. "I've been awake for a long time," she said almost proudly. Guilt pierced his heart. A child needed a good night's rest, a normal routine. Samantha hadn't had any of those since her parents' deaths.

Beth chuckled at the little girl's curiosity. She was so patient, always had time for those in need. And Samantha was in need. "Not sleepy, *kinna*. I'm just sick."

"My mommy and daddy were sick, too. Well, sort of. They died." His heart ached for the child.

According to what they'd been able to ascertain, Trent King, Samantha's father, was one of Bartelli's trusted few. He'd worked as an accountant for the gunrunner and handled the massive amounts of money Bartelli's illegal operation took in each year. Apparently, Bartelli trusted Trent and considered him to be family. Samantha even referred to Lucian as Uncle Lucian. He'd often shared meals with them.

Yet when large amounts of money went missing, Bartelli became convinced only one person could be responsible. According to Samantha, her mother grabbed her and put her into the closet before Bartelli forced his way into their home. Patty King warned her daughter not to make a sound and to stay put no matter what. The young girl had watched through the slats in the closet door as another man held her mother while Lucian shot first Trent and then Patty.

According to Samantha, Lucian had mentioned they needed to find her, but something had stopped him before he could finish searching the house. It was Mason's belief he may have heard some noise outside and feared he would be discovered and fled. Whatever the cause, it had saved Samantha's life.

Once Bartelli and his man left, she ran to the neighbors, who called the police.

A sound behind Mason grabbed his attention

and he spun toward it, his finger on the holstered weapon. His nerves were strung tight.

Erik stood in the doorway, leaning heavily against its frame. "I thought I'd best introduce myself." He managed a weak smile while holding his injured side. "Seemed only right since I'm staying at your home," he told Beth.

Mason resisted the urge to help his partner into the room. Erik would want to operate on his own steam for as long as possible.

As Mason watched his partner slowly advance to Beth's side, doubts returned full force. Had he made the right decision leaving Willa and Erik here as the only real line of defense?

"We'll be all right," Erik assured him. Partners and friends, they knew each other well and thought the same way on most things. Erik would have put himself in Mason's place and come to the same conclusion.

As he reached Beth's bed, Erik held out his hand. "Erik Timmons. Thank you for giving us a safe place to stay."

Beth clasped his hand. "Beth Lambright. You're more than welcome. A friend of Mason's is always welcome here."

"Thank you, ma'am." Erik tussled Samantha's blond hair in an affectionate move that Mason had seen him do with his own kids many times. Both marshals had connected to

Samantha and her story from the start and had let her case become personal with good reason. He and Erik had dealt with their fair share of difficult witnesses through the years, but most had joined the witness protection program because they were in some way involved with a crime. Samantha had done nothing wrong.

"I appreciate you being so generous," Erik responded.

Samantha surprised them by climbing onto Beth's bed, her curious eyes skimming Beth's face. When Mason started to get her down, Beth stopped him. "Leave her be. She's fine."

It tugged at Mason's heart to see the way Samantha seemed to take to Beth right away. The little girl didn't understand the ravages of a disease that gnawed at Beth's life. She only saw a kind woman who she trusted. For a child that craved kindness, Beth proved a true blessing.

"I should hurry," he told them, "while I've still got the element of darkness to stay hidden. It should work in my favor, but it won't last." Mason placed his hand on Samantha's shoulder. "Why don't you stay here with Beth and Golden Boy and keep them company until Beth gets sleepy? Erik and Willa will be just down the hall if you need anything."

The young girl leaned against Beth and asked, "Why are your hands shaking?"

Beth motioned for him not to intervene. She obviously understood the question didn't come from a place of malice.

Mason gave Samantha a hug and hoped he'd see her again.

While Erik and Willa left the room, he stood in the doorway watching Beth with Samantha for a moment longer. The two would be good for each other.

Beth noticed him watching and shooed him away. With a smile, he waved and stepped out of the room.

As he walked down the hall, the reality of the situation struck him head-on. Would he have time to reach the phone before Bartelli's men found him? Or, worse, came back here?

Breathing heavily, Erik dropped into the rocker near the fire. The simple effort of walking to the living room must have greatly depleted his energy.

He opened his eyes as Mason approached. "I just need a moment. Don't worry—Willa and I can handle things here. You get us help."

Mason kept his misgivings to himself. "How many rounds do you have in your clip?" Both he and Erik carried extra clips, but they'd used up plenty defending themselves near the road. Mason was on his backup already.

"Half a clip left and another full one in my pocket."

If forced into another shoot-out, those wouldn't last long.

"Let me help you harness the buggy." Willa pointed to his injured shoulder.

The throbbing made doing the simplest task a challenge—a constant reminder he would be at a disadvantage.

"All right," he agreed, because it had been a while since he'd performed the task. Getting to the phone shanty, making the call and returning before Bartelli's men came back was critical.

"*Gut.* I will get some of *Daed*'s old clothes for you." Her smile took him back in time. She always had the loveliest smile.

Once Willa had disappeared down the hall, Mason knelt beside his partner. "Before I leave, let me check the bandage to make sure you're not bleeding again."

Erik unbuttoned his shirt slowly, each painstaking movement making him flinch. Mason eased the shirt away from the wound so he could get a better look. Blood had soaked through the covering.

"That'll need a clean bandage. Hang tight,

I'll be right back." He tried not to show his concern. Erik leaned his head back against the rocker without answering.

In the kitchen, Mason dug around until he found where Willa had hidden the medical supplies from earlier. He found a clean bandage, grabbed what he'd need to secure the wound and went back to the living room. Though Erik put on a brave front, Mason could see he didn't feel good. What if Erik's condition worsened after he left?

He did his best to replace the bandage without hurting his friend. Still, Erik clamped down on his bottom lip during the process.

"Thank you," Erik whispered in a raspy tone once Mason had finished. He wiped perspiration from his forehead. "I sure hope we're wrong about there being a mole within the marshals service, because if not, there isn't a safe place around where we can protect Samantha from Bartelli."

A crackle of unease shot between Mason's shoulders. "Me, too, brother."

Willa returned with some of her dad's old clothes and Mason used her bedroom to quickly change into the garments. Wearing clothes that had once been part of his everyday life now seemed foreign and awkward. Too many years had passed since he'd dressed Amish.

Once ready, he returned to the living room where Willa had lit one of the lanterns hanging on the wall to provide light for Erik. She held another in her hand.

Willa hurried to the kitchen and returned with a house key. "You should lock the door behind us. I will use my key to get inside."

Erik rose with a groan and went with them to the door. "Be careful, brother. This is a bad situation. Don't get yourself killed."

His partner's remarks drove home with graphic clarity the dangers outside the house. "Don't worry about me. As soon as the buggy is ready, Willa will come back here. Rest, my friend. Hopefully, this will all be over soon, and we'll be on our way with Samantha to put Bartelli away for good."

Erik managed a smile. "I sure hope you're right, but you and I both know what Bartelli is capable of doing."

He did. The photos from Samantha's crime scene showed the extent of Bartelli's anger. Just one example of the crimes Bartelli had allegedly committed.

Mason and Willa stepped out into the rainy morning still shrouded in darkness, and Erik closed the door and slid the lock into place.

Mason turned to the brave woman at his side. "Stay close to me." He didn't know how to explain the bad feeling that wouldn't go away. Willa nodded. And they stepped from the porch and started toward the barn.

"The phone shanty will be easier to reach by road, but it will take longer. It might be better to head to my *Englischer* neighbor's home. He has a phone."

He considered the suggestion. Willa's family fields were behind the house. With the rain continuing, the mare might struggle over the soggy ground. But with the phone shanty on the other side of the mountains, getting there would take time.

The hackles on the back of his neck continued to remind him to be cautious. Tread quietly.

While he ran through the best course of action in his head, Willa suddenly extinguished the lantern without warning and grabbed his arm.

She leaned in close and whispered, "Someone's in the woods in front of the house. They are coming this way. I pray they didn't see the light."

He glanced back at the house. They were closer to the barn. Taking Willa's hand, he hurried toward the building, hoping they would have time to reach it before the intruders spotted them.

Bartelli's people were being cautious, moving through the woods without the benefit of flashlights.

He and Willa were almost to the door when branches snapped beneath the weight of more than one footstep. The men were almost right on top of them and blocking the entrance to the barn. Making it back to the house undetected was impossible. If they stayed here, they'd both be dead.

Willa's blood rushed to her ears while fear threatened to render her immobile. They couldn't stay here. Her brain churned out ways to escape. The thought of another run-in terrified her. Why were they coming back to the house, anyway? Had they realized she'd been dishonest?

Her *daed*'s old wagon. Still holding Mason's arm, she started around the side of the barn toward where her father's work wagon slowly wasted away from lack of use. Though the fog helped to keep them hidden, covering their footsteps would be impossible.

Reaching the wagon, Willa lifted a corner of the thick black tarp she'd placed over the wagon last winter in an attempt to do what she could to protect it. Getting into the back of the wagon with an injured arm proved a challenge Mason couldn't manage alone. Willa did her best to assist him before she scrambled inside. Their ascent wasn't silent. She tugged the tarp back into place and lay lengthwise beside Mason on the wagon's floor.

Fear and exertion accelerated her pulse. Not for a minute did she think those men would hesitate to kill them.

Every little sound near the wagon had her wondering if the men had discovered their hiding place despite her attempts at concealing it.

Voices filtered through the tarp. The men were close. Willa reached for Mason's hand. He entwined his fingers with hers and turned his head toward her. Though the darkness prevented her from seeing his expression clearly, having him close made her feel less afraid. The Mason she knew as a kid would have found this threat just as terrifying as she. The *Englischer* version of that boy had probably dealt with situations far worse.

Samantha's face came into her thoughts. The love Mason had for the child was clear. He'd be her strong protector, fighting to the death to save that little girl.

Mamm believed nothing happened by chance. She saw *Gott*'s hand in every single decision—in everything, *gut* or bad. Had *Gott* orchestrated the events from thirteen years earlier for this moment? For this little girl?

A noise nearby had her heart jumping to her throat. She clutched Mason's hand tighter when the wagon moved slightly as if someone had leaned against it.

"I'm telling you they aren't here. We're miles away from the crash site." The male voice sounded familiar and far too close, as if he were standing right beside the wagon.

"Yeah, well, I saw a light, and what about the footsteps we were tracking? They led to this house, to the porch. Personally, I think that woman lied."

Willa froze. If he believed she hadn't been truthful, would he and the other men return to the house?

"She's Amish, they don't lie," the familiar voice said. This was the man who had spoken to the leader after they'd searched her house. The second man could be one of the two who hadn't said anything. "Anyway, it doesn't matter because he expects us to search every square inch of this place until we find them. They're both injured and they don't have a vehicle." The man sounded annoyed with his partner. "I've heard what he did to that little girl's parents. And to others. I'm not crossing him."

"Were you there?" The second man seemed almost in awe. "Man, that was messed up."

"No, but I was told about it. And it's what he'll do to us if we let these marshals get away with the kid," the first man said.

"I heard he had someone from the marshals service on his payroll. Sooner or later, they'll reach out to their commander and let him know where they're hiding. We can wait around until they contact their people and the guy on the inside lets us know where to find them."

Willa jerked her head toward Mason and clamped down on her bottom lip to keep from making a sound. He didn't appear surprised by what the men were discussing...almost as if he'd known someone from his own agency was working for the man trying to kill Samantha.

"If they're dead, they won't be reaching out to anyone. We've got to find that little girl and take care of her once and for all. You know he's on his way here now."

He? Who was the man talking about? Mason said Lucian Bartelli was being held in jail until his trial.

Willa's staccato pulse ticked off every second that passed in silence. After what felt like forever, the two men seemed to move away.

"I think they've left," Mason said in a low voice. Still, Willa couldn't move.

"Did you know Bartelli had someone inside your agency working for him?"

He exhaled, then nodded and held her gaze. "Let's just say I suspected as much. That's how they keep finding where we're hiding Samantha."

Which meant there would be no help coming from Mason's people.

"Who do you think they were talking about coming here?"

Mason shook his head. "I have no idea. Law enforcement has not been able to identify who this person is. But my guess is, the man who is reportedly Bartelli's second-in-command… and the person Samantha saw. Bartelli rarely handles executions himself, which proved how enraged he had to be with Samantha's father. The man betrayed him when Bartelli considered him a friend. He wanted to handle the execution personally." He told her about how close Samantha's father had worked with Bartelli as his accountant.

"He usually has someone who handles the dirty work for him. Unfortunately, we haven't been able to find out anything about this man beyond that Bartelli trusts him." He quieted for a beat, seeming to listen for any out of the ordinary sounds. "We've managed to arrest a few of Bartelli's people before. Few talk, but from those who have, we've learned this man, who they call Ombra—or shadow—is far worse than Bartelli ever could be."

Willa shivered as Mason eased himself toward the back of the wagon and lifted the tarp enough to see their surroundings. "It's too risky to try to leave with them so close. We'll have to wait until they've cleared out of the area. I don't see anyone." He slowly jumped down and held out his uninjured hand for her. She took it and climbed from the wagon.

All Willa could think about was the men combing the woods near her home. With so many out there, how could they hope to get help for Erik and Samantha?

"Did you recognize either of those voices?"

She had. "Yes, one for sure. They both were probably part of the group that forced their way into the house. They don't appear to be leaving."

She couldn't stop shaking and Mason seemed to realize it. He tucked her closer to his side. The fog had most everything obscured beyond a few feet and made it impossible to judge the distance to the house.

Willa clasped Mason's hand once more. His

warm one encompassing hers helped her feel less afraid.

It was impossible not to make any noise as they crossed the soaked grass. Willa kept her attention on their surroundings, expecting armed men to jump out of the fog before they reached the house.

"Things will work out," Mason murmured as if sensing her fear. But would they? She tried to keep her faith stronger than her doubts.

Sound became distorted in the weather. The rain soaked her prayer *kapp*. Her clothes clung to her skin.

"I heard something," a voice called from ahead.

She stopped dead in her tracks. One of the men. He appeared to be near the front of the house.

"The barn. It's our only chance," Mason whispered against her ear. With her hand tucked in his, they ran while her skirt tangled around her legs.

"Over there. I heard something," the same man said.

"Yeah, I did, too. I just hope it's a person and not a bear."

The barn appeared through the fog, but the men were too close.

"Go check it out," the first man said.

"Me? Why should I go? Why not you?"

The two were arguing and hopefully distracted enough not to see her and Mason.

They kept coming. The first man clearly didn't like his partner's response. "What's the matter?" he taunted. "You afraid?" When his partner didn't respond, he said, "All right, come on. We'll both go."

Willa's heart pumped adrenaline into her body as footsteps crunched along the soggy grass. There was no time to take cover in the barn. And no place to hide.

FOUR

Mason pointed at the woods behind the barn. The tree coverage would give them a chance to stay hidden. Hopefully, the others would think the noise came from a stray animal and give up the search.

Reaching the first of the lodgepole pines, he ducked behind it along with Willa. Mason caught his breath and listened. Not a sound. Where had they gone?

He peeked around the edge of the tree. Nothing moved in his limited visual. Had they given up already? His stomach tightened—a warning to keep on his toes.

If they could stay hidden and circle around behind the house, Willa could use her key to get them inside using the rear door.

Mason whispered his plan against Willa's ear. Before he could put it into action, one of the men entered his line of sight.

He pulled Willa closer and hugged the tree

while the man moved past them and continued deeper into the woods. Where had the partner gone?

Mason's foot connected with a twig on the ground and he cringed as he eased them away from their position.

"Is that you, Jake?" the man called out. Mason inched to where he could see better. The man had his weapon held out in front of him. "You say there are bears in these woods?" The uneasiness in his voice made it clear he didn't want to run into one.

After another moment passed, the man continued moving forward. The missing partner worried Mason the most. They'd been together a few minutes earlier, so where had the second guy gone?

Once the man disappeared into the trees, Mason let Willa go. "We have to hurry." He turned and came face-to-face with the second guy.

"There you are, Marshal." The man's eyes glinted as he aimed the handgun at them. Mason couldn't let him get a shot off and warn his partner as well as the others.

Grabbing for the handgun, he slammed his full weight into his adversary, forcing him to stumble backward. Mason didn't let up.

"Help," the man called to his partner. Mason

quickly reacted, wrapping his arm around the man's throat and squeezing while Bartelli's man struck him with the gun. Mason somehow dodged a direct blow to his head. The man's efforts weakened and the handgun hit the ground as he passed out. But not before alerting his partner.

"Run, Willa."

Taking her hand, he led her through the woods before the second man could reach his unconscious partner.

"Jake, where are you?" the conscious man called out.

The trees grew thick on this part of the property. That, along with the fog, should make it hard for Bartelli's man to see them unless he followed the noise they made running through the woods.

In the soupy darkness, Mason spotted the ruins of the former house that had been on the property many years back when another family owned the land.

"Over there." He urged Willa in front of him, and she headed for the house. Mason glanced behind them, but he couldn't see anything. By now, the second man would have reached his unconscious buddy. Did the guy have time to awaken?

He and Willa reached the structure that consisted of little more than four walls. He hurried her around the side and toward the back. If they kept going in this direction, they'd reach the house.

His biggest fear was that Bartelli's people had called in the attack. If so, there would be no going for help. The house would be surrounded in no time. And not a single person besides Bartelli and his men would ever know what truly happened.

"What do we do now?" Willa asked, her heart rate accelerated. She wasn't used to running for her life.

"By now, those two know Erik and Samantha are inside the house. Keeping them from kicking in the door isn't going to be easy. We have to hurry. I just hope they didn't call this in."

She understood what he meant. If they had alerted others, then time was running out.

Staying close to Mason, Willa eased herself forward. Hopefully, with the weather and darkness, they could lose the men tracking them.

They hurried along the back side of the ruins. Her home was still some distance. "Where are they?"

"Hang on." Mason peeked around the wall of the ruins. "I don't see anyone," he said once he'd returned to her side. "We don't have a choice. Let's keep going." Mason still held her hand. A chill sped through her body as she and Mason stepped from the coverage of the wall and started walking at a fast pace. Willa frequently looked over her shoulder because she couldn't let go of the feeling that their trackers wouldn't be fooled so easily.

The ground around them was littered with dead leaves and tree branches, making it impossible to move quietly. She was relieved when they reached the next group of trees.

"Hang on a second." Mason gathered her behind him and squinted in the direction they'd come. "Is it possible we lost them in the weather?"

Her worst fear was that the men had given up on them and returned to the house. "What if they aren't following us anymore?" She told him her concerns.

"I sure hope that doesn't happen. Stay in front of me and keep your eyes open. We have to be getting closer to your home." He waited for her to lead the way, using his body as protection against a stray bullet. Willa quickly picked her way through the trees while her fears continued to grow. As a child, she'd once played in these woods, never imagining something so deadly would take place here one day.

Mason suddenly grabbed her arm and she froze. Turning her toward him, he placed a finger over his lips and pointed to a nearby tree. They slipped behind it and listened.

Voices in the distance appeared to grow fainter. It sounded as if the men had lost them and were heading away from the farm. Willa exhaled a huge sigh of relief. "They aren't heading toward the house."

"It doesn't appear so. Still, I'll feel better once we're out of sight."

Close to the path that led to her yard, something caught Willa's attention. She stopped and faced Mason. "I heard something."

"I did, too." The words cleared his lips just as a snapping sound—like footsteps crunching leaves—resounded through the woods.

She gathered air into her lungs. Silence returned to the countryside. "Maybe an animal?" she ventured hopefully.

"Maybe." But the doubt in his tone didn't give her confidence. "Either way, we can't stay here."

Mason checked the woods around them as best he could. "I don't see anything. Still, I'll feel better once we reach the house. Stay behind the trees as much as possible." He urged her along to the next group of lodgepole pines.

No voices. No footsteps besides theirs. Still,

Willa couldn't settle down. Those people had everything to lose if they failed. They wouldn't give up so easily.

The clearing to the house appeared in front of them. Just a little bit farther. She and Mason reached the edge of the yard. Her foot touched the grass as two weapons simultaneously discharged, breaking the silence. The men were right on top of them, had probably tracked them all along, waiting for a clear shot.

"We'll never outrun them in time to reach the house." Mason returned their fire and ducked behind a tree.

If they didn't reach the house in time, it would be just him against the men who were determined to take them out. If they were killed, who would protect her mother, Erik and Samantha? Who would fight for that blameless little girl who had already lost so much to Bartelli and his criminal ways?

FIVE

Whether he liked it or not, the choice had been taken from him when the first shots were fired—Mason would have to deal with the two men before the rest of Bartelli's people came to their aid.

It wouldn't take the others long to pinpoint the location of the shots. But if Mason could take both men down quickly and get them out of sight, perhaps Bartelli's soldiers might not realize the shooting had come from Willa's place. Right now, time was of the essence.

"Go around to the back of the house and get down low," he whispered close to Willa while bullets continued to be fired at them.

"No, Mason. They'll kill you." She clutched his arm, her beautiful green eyes holding his. She didn't want to leave him. Just like Willa to try to protect him.

"Listen to me. I'm going to try to disable them so we can tie them up. Go to the back of the house and stay out of sight." He gave her a gentle nudge and returned fire.

Once he could no longer see her, Mason kept a group of trees between himself and his trackers and moved parallel to the left side of the house without being spotted.

A dark silhouette appeared in the yard and started up the porch steps. Where had the second man gone?

Mason steadied himself. "Stop right there." The man whirled toward Mason and fired. He managed to dodge the bullet as it flew past his head. A muffled silence followed by ringing were the results of temporary hearing loss.

Like it or not, if he wanted to live, he'd have to take a life. Mason didn't hesitate. A single shot dropped his assailant where he stood.

Mason shook his head. While his ears still rang from the close shot, at least his hearing had returned.

Movement out of the corner of his eye alerted him to the danger his temporary hearing loss opened him up to. Something slammed into him full force. The second man had found him.

"I got you now, lawman." A smile of triumph was the last thing Mason saw before he hit the ground hard and slammed against his injured shoulder. Mason fought to keep the scream inside.

The man's angry expression hovered inches above him, the gun almost touching his face. "Where's the girl? Is she inside?" Anger turned into a smug smile as Mason's silence confirmed the truth. "She is, isn't she?" The man pulled back the hammer of the weapon.

Mason had somehow managed to hold on to his gun, but his hand had become pinned to his side. If he could get it free...

Desperate, Mason slugged his attacker with his injured arm. An electrical current of hurt raced from the injured shoulder. His attacker's head shot sideways. The force wasn't enough to get the man off him, but he did manage to get his weapon freed.

"You're gonna pay for that," the guy growled, taking aim again. The look of triumph quickly changed to shock when he spotted Mason's weapon.

A single shot slammed the man's eyes shut and he collapsed on top of Mason like a ton of bricks. The effort of keeping himself alive had exacted a toll.

Dragging in air, Mason tried to shove the man off him but the hand-to-hand combat he'd been forced to engage in had wiped out his strength.

"Mason!" Willa rolled the man off him. She

wrapped her arms around his waist and helped him up.

"Are you *oke*?" Her green eyes searched his face with a worried frown.

He'd survived the attacks. "I think so." He glanced back at the two dead men and struggled to come up with the next step. "Let's get them out of sight. There's no way others didn't hear the shooting. When they come to investigate, we can't let them find these two." Bartelli's men would most likely figure out exactly what happened here, but right now, getting these guys out of sight was the best chance they had.

Willa clasped her arms around her body as she looked at the two bleeding from fatal wounds. "I recognize them from the house earlier. They were part of the ones who forced their way inside." She tore her gaze away from the dead men. "We can hide them in the wagon."

He wiped perspiration from his forehead. "That's a good idea." Mason searched the first man's pockets. No identification, but he did have a cell phone that had suffered some damage. If Mason could get it operational again, making the trip to the phone shanty wouldn't be necessary.

The second man had even less on him. No cell phone and no ID.

Before he and Willa could move the first man, the door opened and Erik staggered out onto the porch.

"What happened?" he asked when he spotted the dead men.

Mason explained quickly. "Willa and I will get them out of sight."

"Let me help." Yet Erik held on to the railing and swayed, his legs unsteady.

Though a true hero, Erik was in no shape to lift a body.

"We've got this, brother. Take care of Beth and Samantha."

Erik seemed to realize his limitations and nodded. He grabbed on to the door for support and headed inside.

Seeing his partner so weak terrified Mason, but he tried to keep it to himself.

They carried the two men to the wagon.

"How long before the others come to check on the shots?" Willa asked once the task was finished.

"Not long. They can't be that far away."

"I still can't believe anyone would go to such extremes to hurt an innocent child," Willa told him.

That was something Mason would never understand, either, no matter how many times he faced such darkness.

"Lucian Bartelli has a multimillion-dollar gun-smuggling business that's in jeopardy. If he goes to jail, someone else will take control. He can't afford to let that happen. The people who work under him are living in fear now. The man's temper is notorious."

"How could anyone work for a man like that?"

Mason skimmed her face and wished he could turn back time to the point where he saw the world through Willa's eyes.

"Most are hardened criminals themselves. They have no moral compass, and they are beguiled by the lure of easy money.

"Bartelli's great-grandparents actually came from Italy with extraordinarily little. The grandfather worked hard for an oil company and became quite successful there. He later bought out the company he worked for. His son still owns the business. Bartelli's sister is the CEO. Under her control, they've taken over several failing companies. Bartelli's brother is a high-priced criminal attorney who has been defending his brother through all his previous run-ins as well as this murder trial." Mason shook his head. He didn't understand how Lucian had gone down the wrong path.

"How many other convictions has Bartelli beat?"

Mason hated that someone like Bartelli could still be walking free after the terrible things he'd done.

"Several. He's been accused of murdering others before, but he always managed to wiggle out of it by hiring killers to take care of witnesses." Mason glanced over at the wagon. "Like these two men. I'm sure if I knew their names and ran them, they would have a string of crimes attached to them."

"How do we fight so many?" Willa whispered. "How do you do this every day?"

He couldn't imagine the person she still believed him to be. He'd lost that man a long time ago. The job had changed him radically. Made him harder. Less trusting. A lot jaded.

At one time, he and Willa shared everything with each other. They'd been better friends than he and Miriam, even though Willa was two years younger than him. They'd lived a life of simplicity here in the shadow of the mountains. One centered in faith. How far he'd come from that time!

"It isn't easy," he muttered with a catch in his voice. "There are times when I hardly remember the boy who lived here." The shock on her face wasn't a surprise. She probably couldn't imagine any other way of life. "Let's get to the house before the rest of Bartelli's people arrive."

Their efforts had depleted his waning energy. He needed rest and a plan. Not necessarily in that order.

With Willa close at his side, they started for the front of the wagon—until he spotted a dreadful sight. The two dead men's partners had come to investigate the shooting.

Mason pointed to the danger and ushered her to the back of the wagon and out of sight while the heartbeat in his ears battled with the ringing.

Crouching low, Mason hoped the men wouldn't check their way. If they did, he'd have to take them down and he wasn't sure he had the strength.

Daylight had just begun to turn the darkness to a gloomy gray. Rain continued to fall. The fog had lifted from the farm and remained low on the mountains.

"The gunshots definitely came from this direction." A familiar sound came much closer than Mason liked. It was the man he'd heard calling the shots when he'd been in the basement.

Willa moved closer. He held her against his

side and tried to recall how many men had cut them off on the road. At least half a dozen. By now they probably had more combing every square inch of the territory surrounding the mountains.

Their only chance of survival would be to stay hidden long enough for these men to leave the homestead. He sure hoped he could get the phone working enough to make a call. The alternative meant leaving Willa alone with so many out there. It was an option he couldn't afford to take, which left but one choice—evacuating everyone in the house. A last resort if the phone failed.

"This place appears exactly as we left it," the same man said. "Still, those shots were close. Are you sure you searched that barn properly?" He sounded doubtful.

"Yes, sir. Nothing in there but a couple of animals and a whole lot of stink."

What sounded like a growl came from the leader. "Then where are our missing people?" There was a touch of uneasiness in the tone.

"I don't see any sign of them here, boss," the second man responded. Mason eased himself to the side enough to get his target in sight. Just the two men. If it came to it, he wasn't strong enough to take both men in a fight. He'd be forced to shoot and bring more of Bartelli's people this way.

One of the men turned slightly toward the wagon, and Mason quickly ducked back and cringed. He hoped he hadn't given away their location. Seconds ticked by while he held his breath.

"There's only those two women in the house," the leader said. "I doubt they'd be shooting at anything." An audible sigh followed. "Noise carries in the mountains and this weather isn't helping. Let's keep moving. Whatever you do, don't let down your guard. Those marshals will be watching for us, as well. We need to take them and the girl down quickly. We both know what's at stake. They can't get away this time. The boss's freedom is on the line and he isn't the type to show forgiveness if we fail. Neither is the other one, for that matter. If the boss goes down, we all go down."

Willa's troubled gaze latched on to Mason's face. He drew her closer and wondered exactly who was this person they spoke about. Was this the man known only as Ombra? It made sense Bartelli would send his trusted enforcer to handle the situation.

Mason waited until the men's footsteps grew faint before he slowly eased himself to a standing position and looked around in the early dawn.

He knelt beside Willa once more. "Let's give them a chance to put space between us before we start back."

Waiting didn't come easily with so much at stake. The seconds seemed to pass in slow motion while he tried to shut out all the dreadful things he'd read about Lucian Bartelli's victims. The man didn't appear to possess a conscience. He'd started his life of crime early on. When his younger brother went away to college, Bartelli began smuggling weapons into the US to sell to street gangs. Why hadn't someone from Bartelli's family seen the problem and tried to get him back on track? According to everything Mason had read about the family, the Bartellis were law-abiding people.

Leaving the way of life you'd grown up with proved easy for some. Look at Mason. He'd come from a Plain family dominated by faith, yet he'd traveled so far from that life that he barely recognized himself anymore.

He shoved his regrets down deep. Feeling sorry for himself wasn't going to help Samantha.

Mason slowly rose. "I think it's safe." He helped Willa up beside him while his thoughts chased after each other. Getting the damaged phone to work had become key, because if he had to evacuate Erik, Samantha and Beth with so many men combing the countryside, he feared there would be no way to avoid another shoot-out.

Together, they moved toward the house while he searched their surroundings, expecting more of Bartelli's soldiers at any moment. So far, it was only him and Willa. Still, he tempered each step to be as quiet as possible. Just a few more to go. The simple white house with its fading paint had never looked so welcoming.

For the time being, Bartelli's people didn't suspect Willa and Beth of hiding them. He hoped it stayed that way, but he'd heard them say Bartelli would kill them if they failed. The promise of certain death could be a strong motivator.

Through the curtains she and *Mamm* had lovingly sewn, Willa noticed the glow of the fire in the stove and the soft light from the lanterns in the living room and kitchen. They were safe.

She wanted to run up the steps and throw open the door, to lock the nightmare away for *gut*. But she had a feeling it wouldn't leave so easily. Bartelli's men were ruthless criminals like their boss, all determined to stay out of jail at any cost.

Before she had the chance to climb the stairs, something on the ground caught her attention. Among the spent shells from Mason's gun battle, blood had soaked the soggy grass.

"How did those men not notice the shell casings?" she asked.

"My guess is they were too busy trying to find their partners and us that they failed to look at the ground."

Mason gathered the spent shells in his pocket. "There's nothing we can do about the blood. The rain should take it away soon enough." He glanced uneasily around the farm before ushering her up the steps.

Willa's fingers shook as she brought out the key.

Being out here in the open after everything they'd gone through felt as if both she and Mason had glaring targets on their backs.

She slipped the key into the lock. Inside the house, the sound of footsteps headed their way. Willa opened the door and noticed Erik standing nearby. Mason followed her inside and quickly relocked it.

The reality of what they'd survived settled in. Her hands shook and her stomach churned.

Two people were dead, and it wasn't close to being over.

Mason told Erik about the men who had shown up. "They were looking for their partners. They've left for now."

"We've got to find a way to get Samantha out of here before the place becomes surrounded. There won't be any way out for us then." Erik eased himself back to the rocker and slowly lowered his frame.

Mason pulled out the phone he'd stuck in his pocket. "I'm not sure how long we'll have if Bartelli's people find their dead partners." He held up the phone. His biggest concern was that with Bartelli being so paranoid, he might have placed some type of tracking software on the phone, but at this point, they needed some way to reach out for help. It was a risk he'd have to take. "One of the men had a phone on him. It's busted up, but I'm going to see if I can get it working again."

Erik barely acknowledged what he'd said.

"How are you holding up, partner?" Mason asked, putting the busted phone aside.

"I'm hanging on," Erik mumbled almost indistinguishably. "Just going to rest for a second."

"Let's get you to the sofa where you'll be

more comfortable," Willa said as she studied Erik's slouched frame.

Mason moved to Erik's side. "Hang on to me." Draping Erik's arm around his neck and placing his own around his wounded friend, Mason lifted him. Willa moved to the opposite side to help. Working together, they slowly walked Erik to the sofa.

He groaned in pain as his injured side struck the sofa.

"I'm sorry," Willa whispered when he stumbled. "We should check the bandage again."

Mason slowly unbuttoned his partner's shirt and examined the bandage. "It seems to be holding up so far." He closed Erik's shirt while Willa brought over a quilt and draped it over him. "Is Samantha still with Beth?" Erik managed a nod. Mason continued to stare at his wounded partner. The love he had for his friend was clear on his troubled face.

"He'll be *oke* for a little while. He needs rest. Let's see if we can get the phone working again."

Mason turned toward her. It hurt to see the hopeless look on his face. It reminded her of that young man who had lost his best friend all those years ago. Mason and Chandler Sweitzer had been *gut* friends since they were *kinner*. They'd gone ice skating the winter before

Mason left the community and Chandler had fallen through the ice. Mason hadn't been able to save his friend and for that he'd blamed himself. She still remembered this same look on his face when he'd come to her house and told her about Chandler.

"*Komm*, I will make us some *kaffe* to warm up."

With a final look Erik's way, Mason came with her to the kitchen. He pulled out a chair and placed the busted phone on the table to examine. "I'm worried about him, Willa. Erik has a wife and family. They need him. If I can't get this thing working, how can I leave you here to face Bartelli's men alone should they return? But if I don't, my partner might die. The alternative is forcing everyone into the buggy." He shook his head. "There is no easy solution. Someone will be at risk no matter what."

Willa came over to where he sat and put her arms around him. This was Mason. Her friend. She cared about him and she would do whatever possible to help him figure out the best course of action.

She leaned back and looked into his eyes. "We'll find a way. *Gott* will help us."

A hard look replaced the worry. He'd lost his faith. Her heart broke. She would have enough for both of them. "*Gott* will help," she insisted, and touched his face. Willa wished she could do something more, but her ways were not his anymore.

As she continued to look into his eyes, something shifted, and her heart seemed to skip against her chest. Mason gently clasped her wrist, holding her there when she would have stepped back.

She struggled to get enough air into her lungs. The past and all her wishes were right there for him to see. She'd imagined this look on his face so many times, thought about what might have been had Mason loved her instead of Miriam. She'd hated that for a time, and she'd resented Miriam because of it.

"Mason." She didn't recognize her own voice. She should pull free. Move away. Bury those hopes once and for all...but she didn't want to.

They continued to watch each other without saying a word. What was he thinking? She'd give anything to know.

"What are you doing?" A tiny voice intruded into the moment.

Both she and Mason jerked toward the innocent child watching them. Samantha stood in the kitchen entrance rubbing sleep from her eyes while she clutched Benny tight in the crook of her arm.

Mason let Willa go, and she quickly put space between them. He went over to the child and knelt in front of her. "We're working on a phone. Hopefully, I can fix it so we can call for help." He glanced at Willa before turning back to Samantha and asking, "Were you sleeping?"

The little girl nodded. "I heard something. It scared me." Tears hovered in brown eyes that held a wisdom that could only be earned by walking through the trials of life. It went way beyond Samantha's young years.

The gunshots from earlier. Had they triggered a flashback of watching her parents' deaths? Willa's heart hurt for this child who had suffered so much.

Mason gathered Samantha in his arms. "Oh, sweetheart, you're safe here. I made you a promise not to let anything happen to you, and I plan to keep it."

The little girl hiccuped out several sniffles and held on to Mason as if afraid he, too, would be taken from her life.

Gott, please give this innocent kinna *Your peace.*

Mason lifted the child up and sat down in the chair he'd vacated with Samantha clinging to him.

"Hey, dry those tears, sweetheart." He looked up at Willa with a wounded expression, the love he had for little Samantha clear in the way he watched over her.

In the past, Mason always teased Willa about caring for every wounded animal she found, but he was the one who protected them whenever trouble came near. Or when one of his *bruders* tried to do something foolish.

Mason cleared his throat. "Are you hungry?"

The child sniffed a few more times before she pulled away and looked at him. She gave a tiny nod and Mason smiled. "Well, I'm sure Willa can fix you something special. And then maybe you can be my assistant as I work on the phone."

Samantha forgot about her fears for a second and willingly agreed. "I want to fix the phone." She was resting in the promise that Mason gave her.

"That's good, because I can use these little fingers of yours to help me reach what I can't with mine." He held his hand against Samantha's smaller one and she giggled.

Her forehead wrinkled. "You have big hands."

"That's because I'm all grown up and you're still little. And I'm a guy."

"My hands will be big like yours one day. I know they will," the little girl announced proudly.

Mason chuckled and hugged her close. "Well, you're going to have to grow a lot to fit into these big hands." He tugged at her ponytail like he had the strings of both Miriam's and Willa's prayer *kapps* many years ago. Willa smiled at the memory.

Watching the closeness that existed between Mason and this precious child, she wondered about his life. Had he thought about marriage after what happened between him and Miriam? She knew truly little about his life now. Perhaps Mason had met someone special?

As *kinner* growing up in the small community of West Kootenai, she and Mason had shared their hopes and dreams for the future. Most Amish wished for marriage and a family. She and Mason had been no different. She just hadn't realized those wishes would never be hers to claim.

He glanced up and caught her watching him. The questions in his eyes proved he'd seen things she didn't want him to see. Willa turned away and let go of what she'd once hoped for. She thought she'd made peace with never having a husband or *kinner* of her own, yet the ache in her heart said differently. *Mamm* needed her. Willa never had a second thought about caring for the woman who had given up so much for her family.

"I think we could all use something to eat," Willa said, and steadied herself to face Mason again. "I know it's early, but you all must be hungry after what you've been through."

A smile wiped the concern from Mason's face. "Thank you. And yes, we are. It's been a long time since any of us has eaten. Food would be great." He reached for the phone and examined it while the little girl in his lap leaned over close and did the same. The homey picture had Willa turning away and trying not to feel sorry for herself. She led a *gut* life. She had her *mamm* and this beautiful farm her *daed* had worked so hard to build for the family. *Gott* had blessed her beyond what she deserved.

Once the threat facing Mason and Samantha passed, he would leave. Her life would return to normal. She would take each day that *Gott* gave her and be happy.

She watched Mason with Samantha and swallowed back regret. Not hers to have. Best not to look too long at what might have been. She must focus on the future and be grateful. Those foolish *maede* dreams were before her mother's diagnosis. Before Willa got a glimpse into what her future could be.

SIX

He'd done everything he could think of and yet the phone still wouldn't make a call. Old inadequacies returned full force to remind him that if he let Samantha down now it would mean her life.

Mason set the phone down, keeping up a brave front for the little girl in his lap. Samantha had enough to worry about. Testifying against the man who killed her parents wasn't going to be easy. It would take all her strength.

"Sorry, kiddo, I don't think there's any fixing this one."

Samantha's solemn eyes skimmed his face. "That's okay, Mr. Mason. You'll find another way to get us help." The confidence she had in him reminded him the clock was ticking.

Samantha hopped from his lap and went over to where Willa prepared a tray of food for her mother. The simple grilled cheese sandwich and tomato soup she'd made for him and

Samantha never tasted better. It recharged his energy level and made him feel almost human again. He'd taken food to Erik, but despite the need, his partner had only managed a few spoonfuls of the soup.

Mason sipped his strong black coffee and watched Willa with the little girl. The way she explained her mother's disease in childlike terms for Samantha to understand reminded him of what he'd known for years. She was born to be a mother.

"Can I help?" Samantha asked with her little head tilted to one side in a gesture Mason knew well. Whenever curious, she'd look at Mason the same way.

More than anything, he wanted Samantha to have a bright future. That depended entirely on putting Bartelli away. The child deserved a simple life where she could be surrounded by people who loved her and made her feel safe. The young girl needed someone like Willa, who possessed a caring heart, to guide her into adulthood.

Willa's expression softened as she explained how she must assist her mother with the meal. "I can certainly use an extra set of hands, and I know *Mamm* would enjoy talking with you and Benny some more."

Samantha's eyes lit up and Mason smiled

to himself. Beth had that effect on everyone. The child turned to him. "Can I, Mr. Mason?"

"Of course. Go with Willa. I'll keep working on the phone." It wasn't the truth. There was nothing more he could think to do with the phone. But for however long they were here, and no matter what happened next, he wanted Samantha not to be afraid. If being with Beth and Willa gave her a sense of normalcy and safety, then so be it.

"Why do you call your mother *Mamm*," Samantha asked when Willa handed her a napkin.

"That is our word for *mother*. And thank you for assisting me." She smiled down at the child, whose eyes shone with excitement.

"I can carry those, too." Samantha pointed to the silverware on the tray.

Willa handed them to her. "Yes, you can. *Denki*."

The child grinned up at Mason, flashing a gap between her front teeth where she'd lost one of her baby ones while under his care.

"Look, Mr. Mason. I'm helping."

He chuckled and nodded. "You sure are."

It broke his heart to think of Samantha all alone in the world without any living relatives to take her in. For now, she'd become a ward of the state. Once the trial ended, she'd be put into the foster system. He couldn't imagine her life then. Because of mistakes her father made, this precious child would be forced to pay the price.

"It will be *oke*," Willa whispered as she passed him. Her hand pressed his uninjured shoulder. More than anything he wanted to believe her...but his heavy heart wouldn't allow it. Doubts and fears for Samantha's future ran deep. Worry over his partner warred with them. Sitting here and doing nothing wasn't an option. The longer he waited, the higher the likelihood more of Bartelli's people would arrive and increase the danger to this quiet community that had once been his home. As soon as Willa returned, he'd try again to get the buggy out. Everyone in the house was in danger. If he could get them into the buggy without being spotted, they stood a chance of escaping, but getting a disabled woman and a wounded man out before the enemy arrived wouldn't be easy.

Mason picked up the phone again and removed the back once more, studying it closely. He and Samantha had tried taking the battery out and replacing it, without any change. Mason stared at the phone and sat back in his chair when he recalled something he'd gone through with his personal cell phone a few years back. The phone didn't have service and so he'd been told to remove the SIM card and replace it to reconnect.

He carefully pulled the card out and studied it. It didn't appear damaged. He blew it off and replaced it, then powered the phone up again. This time, it acted like it wanted to work, but the call still wouldn't go through.

He rubbed a frustrated hand across his forehead and stared at the phone a second longer before the truth dawned. The service indicator flashed no signal here in the kitchen.

Jumping to his feet, he almost knocked the chair to the floor. Mason moved around the kitchen, but the service indicator didn't change.

In the living room, he checked several spots without any service. In one corner, he almost had a bar. Mason attempted to make a call. It didn't go through.

He tried the rest of the house but was met with the same result everywhere. Mason knocked on Beth's door and stepped inside. All three females looked his way. Golden Boy apparently considered him a friend because the animal barely lifted its head.

"Sorry to interrupt." Seeing Willa assisting Beth with her meal just about ripped his heart apart. Mason struggled to recover and held up the phone. "We fixed it, Samantha."

The little girl's eyes lit up. "We did?" She

ran over to Mason and wrapped her tiny arms around his waist. "I knew you could do it, Mr. Mason."

He lifted her into his arms and pointed to the service indicator. "See that." He waited for her to spot it.

"I do." Her blond ponytail swished her affirmation.

"Well, good, because that's where we'll see if we have enough service to make a call. Now, you keep your eyes on it and we'll walk around the room. Let me know if it changes."

"I will, Mr. Mason." The little girl didn't look away from the indicator.

Mason carried her around the room. As they reached the last shadowy corner, he realized there would be no service found inside the house.

Like it or not, he'd have to try outside. And if the mountains or the weather were blocking the signal? He didn't want to think about that.

"There aren't any bars." Samantha's expression fell.

"No, not here in the house, but maybe outside. I'll go out and check."

Willa set the spoon down and turned to him. "Let me. They recognized you earlier. They probably have photos of both you and

Erik. They will be expecting to see me around the house."

He shook his head. "It's too dangerous." He didn't like the idea of sending Willa out alone to do his job.

"I want to come, too," Samantha announced.

As much as he loved the little girl, he couldn't let her be in harm's way.

He tugged at her ponytail. "Sorry, kiddo. You have to stay inside and watch out for Ms. Beth and Golden Boy."

The little girl's bottom lip stuck out in a pout. "But I want to help."

Mason's heart melted. "You are. You are going to keep Ms. Beth company and protect her. Why don't you tell her one of the jokes you've told me and Erik?" Mason looked to Beth and winked. "As I recall, Ms. Beth loves jokes."

Beth had been a jokester from way back and loved to play tricks on the kids. She would sneak up behind them and shout, "Boo," or she would tell them a scary tale. He spent many an hour as a young man trying to get her back. That woman still existed in her failing body. The glint in her eyes now proved it.

"I do love jokes," she told the little girl. "And I think you can tell some funny ones."

Mason lowered the child to the floor. She went over to Beth's bedside.

"Why did the chicken cross the road?"

Mason suppressed a chuckle as he stepped out into the hall with Willa. "She has a bunch of jokes just as corny as that one, but I love every one of them."

Before Willa closed the door, she watched Samantha with her mother. "She is precious. I feel so terrible for her. Losing both parents in such a dreadful way, and now having to go through this."

Ever since he'd read Samantha's story, he'd been trying to understand how God could allow such a terrible thing to happen to that guiltless little girl. It wasn't fair. Just like it wasn't fair that He'd taken Chandler's life before his friend ever had the chance to fall in love, get married and have a family of his own.

Barely sixteen and dead because he'd fallen through ice. Remembering that day, Mason could still feel the panic racing through his body like he was back there. He'd tried to get to his friend and save him, yet all of his efforts were in vain. Chandler had died along with a part of Mason's youth that day. The young man with so much hope disappeared. In his place came one filled with anger.

Willa reached for her cloak on the peg near

the front door. After everything that happened already, he didn't want to put her life in jeopardy again. "Willa, I can't let you do this. It's too risky. You've seen what these men are capable of."

She stubbornly shook her head. "That's why I should be the one to try to find service. They don't know their two partners are dead. They expect me to work around the farm. If they catch you by surprise…" She held out her hand and clutched his. "Please, let me do this, Mason. For you and Erik. For Samantha."

"I'll be watching from the window. If anything looks out of place, call out right away."

Though she didn't feel anywhere as confident as she wished, Willa nodded. "I will, don't worry." She tied on her traveling bonnet for added protection against the rain that didn't appear ready to let up anytime soon.

Mason handed the phone to her. "This is what you're looking for. The service indicator bar will rise if you pick up a signal. You'll need at least one bar to make a call. Probably more."

He held her gaze. "If we can't get a signal, we won't have a choice. We'll have to evacuate everyone quickly."

She clutched the phone tight in her gloved

hands and waited until Mason wasn't visible before she opened the door and slipped out.

The rain made it hard to see anything. This far north and close to the mountains, a day like this was common. The mountains had a way of gathering weather around them. While she loved living near them, at times they gave a sense of being isolated from the rest of the community. Just their farm and a handful of *Englischer* ranches.

With *Mamm*'s health issues, Willa wondered how long they would be able to hold on to the farm. Being so far away from the rest of the community made it difficult for the menfolk to get their animals here to help with the crops. Her neighbor Ethan Connors had planted this year, and she was grateful for everything he did for them. Still, she couldn't expect him to do the work when he had plenty of his own.

Willa inhaled deeply and released it into the chilly morning. Stepping from the porch, she glanced over her shoulder to the window. The smallest of movements there made her smile. Having Mason watching nearby gave her a sense of safety.

The phone's light reflected the lack of service. She kept it hidden in her covered hands in case anyone were to happen this way again. They'd think it odd that an Amish woman would possess a phone, and she didn't want to give anything away.

Willa started for the barn first. She wouldn't go inside unless necessary. Staying in view of the living room, she glanced down at the phone. So far, the service bar hadn't moved. As she neared the structure, her eyes darted around the farm. Though she wanted to be brave for Mason and Samantha, these criminals scared her. She'd barely kept it together during their last interrogation. Would she be able to convince them she had no knowledge of Samantha or the marshals should they come upon her again?

Her attention returned to the phone. The indicator bar hadn't budged. What if they couldn't find service?

She changed direction in hopes of picking up something in another spot on the property.

Willa moved to the side of the barn near the wagon. Still nothing. Would Mason be able to see her here? As she debated how much farther to go, a noise in the woods near the back of the house halted her steps. Voices came her way through the drizzly weather. More than one person was heading for the house. She froze briefly before running for the barn. Two men's voices grew closer. As much as she wanted to warn Mason about the danger, if she did, they would hear her.

Willa grabbed the door handle and turned it. The door wouldn't budge. This one rarely saw use and had become warped over time. Another thing she needed to fix before the next winter came upon them.

Putting her shoulder into it, she tried to force it to open. Though only two men spoke, Willa couldn't tell how many were actually tromping through the woods, but it sounded like a lot.

After another try proved useless, Willa gave up and ran to the opposite side of the barn and closer to the advancing men. Would Mason see her? Willa grabbed the handle. Before she could open it and slip inside, someone came up behind her. Willa whirled in time to see Mason standing close. She bit back a scream and covered her trembling mouth.

"Sorry," he mouthed, and pushed the door open. They stumbled inside. Mason quickly closed the door as quietly as possible.

"Do you think they heard us?" she whispered.

"I hope not." He looked around the space. The cow mooed as if expecting her morning meal. Both mares nickered. Would the noise of the animals give away their intrusion? If Bartelli's people heard the animals complaining they'd come inside to investigate. She and Mason had to find a hiding spot quickly.

Daed had built an upper level onto the barn to store hay. A ladder led up to it.

"Up there." Willa pointed to the stacks of hay. "We can hide behind the square bales."

Mason kept watch below until she reached the landing above, then started up the steps.

"There's all sorts of footprints around out here. Look," a voice said close to the door.

Mason scrambled up the rest of the way as the door opened. He ducked down beside her.

The animals continued to complain about the additional intrusion without any food being provided.

"I don't see anyone in here," another man said.

"Still, someone's been around recently. Look at the footprints. Let's take a look around the place before we leave."

"It's probably that Amish woman."

Willa held Mason's gaze and understood what he wished to convey. If the men came up here, they wouldn't have a choice but to shoot them.

Movements could be heard from the ground floor. The cow let out several stressed sounds when the men got too close.

"Filthy animal. Why would anyone want to live like this?" Disgust filled the man's tone.

"They don't know anything else, I guess." The second man sounded close to the ladder. A stair creaked. Willa clutched Mason's arm. They were coming up the ladder. "I'm going to check up here real fast."

She and Mason got as low as they could and away from the view of the stairs.

"All that's up there is a bunch of hay. I say we check the house again."

Please, no. The house wasn't locked. If they went inside, they'd see Erik. They'd find Samantha. She closed her eyes and prayed her heart out to *Gott.*

A footstep hit the landing. Willa bit her bottom lip. If they came a smidgen closer…

"We won't bother the Amish women. Would they be harboring two marshals and a child?" He laughed. "The rest of the team is coming soon. Let's fall back to the road near the edge of this property and wait. Once they arrive, we'll search every square inch of this miserable country if we have to." The man made his way down the ladder. "They're here somewhere."

Sounds of the two moving across the barn were followed by the door opening and closing.

As much as Willa wanted to believe they'd

gone for real, she couldn't move. Not after everything they'd been through. "Is it a trick?"

"I don't think so. They're waiting for others, which means we have to get everyone out of here now. Those two might not want to bother you and Beth, but who knows what the others will do, especially if Ombra shows up here."

Willa pulled out the phone and looked at it. "Still nothing." She shook her head. "Why can't we pick up a signal?"

Mason took the phone from her. "My guess is the weather could be playing havoc with the cell tower. Hopefully, it will affect their communication, as well. That's something." His blue eyes held hers. "Help me get the enclosed buggy ready. We won't have long to get everyone out of the house and away before those men return with an army."

He rose and held out his hand. Once they reached the bottom floor, Mason moved to the door and cracked it as he listened. He turned back to Willa. "I don't hear anything. Let me look around outside to be sure." He stepped out of sight. She stood in the middle of the barn and counted off every second of his absence in her head. When he came back, Willa somehow resisted the urge to hug him.

"There's no sign of them for now."

The chances of them making it to the neighbor's without being spotted would be small, but staying here was no longer an option.

"Let's get the animals tended to as fast as possible. We can't afford not to milk the cow. The animals won't survive without food and water until we can return," Willa told him.

While Mason fed the animals, Willa did her best to milk Buttercup in record time. With the task completed, she led Peppermint out of her stall. Every second it took to get the horse ready had Willa wondering if their efforts would be in vain. Would those two men return before they had the opportunity to leave the property?

Though she'd harnessed Peppermint countless times without thinking about it, her fingers fumbled over the steps. Staying focused on what was necessary became nearly impossible when all she could think about was the danger that could be waiting for her and Mason beyond the door.

She struggled so long with latching the harness strap that Mason took over.

"Here, let me." He quickly finished the job.

"I'll get the milk. Can you open the heavy doors with your arm?"

"I can manage." He did his best not to show any pain, but she could see the way he favored the injured shoulder.

Willa grabbed the pail of fresh milk and placed it inside the buggy while Mason moved to the front and slowly opened the double doors.

"You should guide the mare from the barn. I'll close the doors," she told him.

With her help, Mason made it up to the seat and took up the reins. The glimpse of the gun holstered inside his jacket was another reminder of the danger facing them.

He shook the reins. Willa followed behind until the buggy cleared the doors. Just as she turned to shut them, a sound nearby had her spinning in the direction of the noise.

The mare must have sensed danger, as well, because she nickered loudly while her nostrils flared.

Two men materialized from the side of the barn and Willa bit back a scream. While her heart threatened to jump from her chest, out of the corner of her eye, she noticed Mason climbing from the buggy.

One of the men she recognized from inside her house stepped forward. "Sorry to frighten you, ma'am, but as I told you before, we're looking for some people. Have you noticed any strangers hanging around your property since earlier?" The hard look on his face gave her the creeps. He glanced toward Mason who had eased toward the back of the buggy. Near enough to reach her if there was trouble, but still in the shadows to keep the men from recognizing him.

Willa lifted her chin and prayed the thrashing of her heart couldn't be heard. "There's been no one here. Just you." She noticed a gun peeking out of the man's jacket. No doubt both men were armed.

The man's gaze narrowed at what she'd said. He stepped closer and into her personal space. "I thought you said only you and your mother lived in the house? Who is this?" He eyed Mason suspiciously.

While her body threatened to hyperventilate, Willa struggled to get words out. She made eye contact with Mason. He warned her to stay calm. Easier said than done when facing down armed men.

The man took a threatening step toward Mason while sizing him up. The Amish disguise helped, and Mason had the black felt hat tugged low on his head.

Mason kept his head down and didn't make eye contact. "I'm her husband. There's been no one around the farm. Just me and my wife and her mother."

The man raised his eyebrows, his full attention on Mason now. He stepped closer to get a better look. Recognition immediately turned his frown to shock. "You're one of those lawmen."

The man whipped his weapon out, but Mason beat him to the draw and fired twice. He dropped without getting off a single shot. The second man, fearing the same fate, took off toward the woods while firing wildly.

Willa hit the ground and covered her head as bullets sailed all around her.

Mason hurried over and lifted her to her feet. "Are you hurt?"

"No, I'm fine." But the attack had left her shaken.

"Stay here. I'm going to see if I can capture him before he has a chance to warn the others." Mason ran after the man, who continued shooting at him.

Willa stayed hidden behind the buggy and prayed Mason wouldn't be struck by a bullet.

In the woods separating her place from the road, gunshots were exchanged. They continued for a little while longer and then silence.

Gott, please keep him safe.

A rustling sound from the nearby woods had her ducking low. Someone emerged from the trees and rounded the back of the buggy. Willa pointed the handgun taken earlier from one of the deceased men. Her finger rested on the trigger ready to fire.

Mason stopped short when he spotted it. "It's me, Willa."

She lowered the weapon and exhaled a huge sigh before she dropped the gun and ran into Mason's arms. "I was so sure he'd kill you."

He held her close. "I'm unharmed. I hit him in the side, but he got away. Once he makes his way to his partners, he'll warn the rest of Bartelli's men that we're here." She could feel his heart racing. "That man now knows Samantha's here. How hard will it be for your mother to get into the buggy?"

Willa pulled away and looked at him. "She can't really walk without help."

"I'll carry her. It will be faster. Unfortunately, the journey won't be an easy one. We'll have to travel through the pasture behind your house, and the rain won't make it easy."

The thought of her *mamm*'s frail body bouncing around in the back of the buggy worried her.

He brushed his hand across her cheek. "I'm sorry. I know it's not ideal, but we no longer have the choice. We'll have to find a way to your neighbor's place."

Willa stared at the dead man while a fear that wouldn't go away told her time was critical.

"Let's get the buggy to the house." He reached for the lead rope while Willa grabbed the handgun once more and kept him close. They covered the space between the barn and the house swiftly.

Willa lifted the milk pail and hurried up the steps while Mason tied off the animal and followed. He closed the door and locked it.

She carried the milk into the kitchen and placed it on the table. Willa retrieved the pitcher from the battery-powered refrigerator and filled it, then fumbled around the top cabinet to get the extra pitchers. She stopped. Why was she worried about milk when their lives were in danger?

"Here, let me help you." Mason leaned past her to grab the two pitchers before they landed on her head. He sat them down and slowly faced her. As much as she wished she could hide her fears from him, she couldn't. The difficult circumstances facing them terrified her and he saw it.

"Hey." He gathered her close. "We have a chance."

But she wasn't nearly as certain. Willa struggled to keep her composure. Mason was trying so hard to be strong for her. She had to do the same for him. Giving in to the panic wouldn't help anyone.

"I'm sorry." She shook her head.

His hands cupped her face and he looked into her eyes. "You have nothing to be sorry for. You're doing great. I'm not going to let them hurt you, Willa. I would never let that happen." Something unreadable entered his eyes.

"Do you ever miss this life?" She searched his face and caught a glimpse of the boy she'd once loved.

"More than I can ever say, especially during a case like this. Nothing about it makes sense and it just seems so horrific." He stopped and shook his head. "I wish I could come home to the past I left behind. To this simple world."

The admission filled her with hope she couldn't accept. Willa tamped it down. Mason's future did not involve her. She placed her hand on his arm. "You can. There's no reason why you can't."

His laughter held a brittle quality about it. "I've come too far from this life to go back. I'm not the same person you knew back then. I've done some things."

After witnessing the events of today, Willa understood clearly what Mason's job entailed. She struggled to reconcile the rambunctious boy from the past with the skilled and hardened law-enforcement agent standing before her.

"Nothing is impossible for *Gott*. If you want to return to your Amish faith, *Gott* will make a way. But it must be your decision." She turned away, poured the extra milk into the pitchers and placed them into the refrigerator.

"I wish it were that simple."

She believed him.

"Truth is, I'm not sure I know how to be Amish anymore. And more importantly, I don't deserve to be called Amish."

She rejected his answer with a shake of her head. "You will always be part of this community and part of your family—and mine. Nothing you do or choose will take you from us." She pointed to her heart. "Because you are in here."

SEVEN

He didn't deserve her loyalty. The life he'd chosen went against everything he once believed in.

Mason didn't know how to answer her and so he did what he had for the past thirteen years. He pushed it aside and told himself it was a discussion for another day—when Bartelli no longer posed a threat. Yet the gnawing in his gut assured him that day might never come.

"I'll get Erik ready to travel. Can you prepare Beth for the trip? She'll need some extra blankets to keep warm and to make her comfortable. Bring Samantha now. I'll come back for your mother once Erik is settled."

In the living room, Erik's eyes remained closed. He hadn't moved at all when they'd come in and didn't stir now as Mason knelt beside him. Would his decision to move them all be another mistake? His insecurities had him wavering. How could he leave Willa here to protect three people against so many?

"You weren't able to find any service," Erik murmured, and opened his eyes.

"No, and we're out of options." He explained about the last attack. "Bartelli's men know we're here with Samantha. Staying is no longer an option." He told Erik about what he'd overheard Bartelli's men saying. "I have no idea how many more are coming." He pointed to Erik's side. "That's getting worse. You need proper medical care."

Erik rubbed his damp forehead. "I know. How do we get out of here without a car? I don't want to die here, Mason. Not like this. I can't leave my family."

The admission ripped through Mason. "Hey, that's not going to happen. I won't let it." But at this point, getting them all out safely felt like the fight of his life.

Forced from one safe house after another, he'd had little time to sleep. The effects of the constant running and the tension, as well as being shot, had caught up with him. His energy was almost nonexistent. Thinking clearly took extraordinary strength.

"Willa's family buggy is waiting for us outside. I'm going to help you get there. Willa will bring Samantha and then I'll come back for

Beth." It sounded so easy, but it wasn't anything close and Erik's reaction didn't appear confident.

"Sure, it could work. What choice do we have?" Erik always had his back no matter how desperate the situation they faced.

Mason patted Erik's shoulder. "I'll be right back." He rose and went over to the window.

Outside, the dreary day made visibility around the farm difficult. He struggled to see past the yard. The woods where the man had fled made a natural barrier between the Lambright place and the small road that ran beyond. Bartelli's people could be out there waiting for him to make a wrong move.

Mason slipped into his jacket and grabbed Erik's.

Tucking the weapon he'd taken from the dead man inside his pocket along with the phone, he readied himself for what would follow.

Willa still had the handgun she'd pointed at him earlier. As added protection, he'd take Josiah's shotgun. He rummaged around the kitchen until he found the stash of extra shells. Stuffing them into his pocket, Mason returned to his partner.

"Did you see anyone out there?" Erik murmured so low Mason had to lean close to hear.

"Not so far." He dropped the jacket onto the sofa. "I'm going to help you sit up now." He placed his arm around Erik's shoulders and eased him halfway upright.

Erik groaned and clutched his injury while pain contorted his expression.

"I'm sorry, brother. I know it hurts."

Erik dragged in air. "Just keep going."

Mason did as his brave partner asked and lifted him up to a sitting position.

"It's cold out and I don't know how far we'll have to travel before we have service or reach the rancher's place." Mason didn't like his partner's pallor one little bit. "Can you get your arms in the jacket?" Because he had doubts.

"I think so. I could use some more of those pain meds, though."

Mason watched his partner make several attempts to get his arm through the hole before he helped Erik the rest of the way.

"Thanks. I guess I'm a long way from being a hundred percent." Erik's raspy voice scared him the most.

"You take a break and I'll get the pain meds." He went into the kitchen and looked around for the pills, then shook out a couple once he found them and shoved the bottle into his pocket.

With a glass in hand, he brought the pills to Erik.

"Thanks." Erik closed his eyes and laid his head against the back of the sofa.

He felt his partner's forehead. The fever had spiked. Erik was burning up.

Mason hurried to the kitchen and grabbed a cloth. He dampened it with cool water and placed it on Erik's forehead.

How could they leave with Erik in such bad shape? He required a doctor's care before the wound became infected.

Mason noticed fresh blood seeping through his partner's shirt. The wound had opened back up.

He knelt in front of Erik. "You're bleeding. I need to change the bandage before we go." Erik's lack of response had him wondering if the decision to evacuate would come too late to save his partner...

Willa stared down at the child who had snuggled up against *Mamm*'s side and fallen fast asleep.

"I hope I don't have to wake her." If this *kinna* kept right on sleeping, it would be a blessing from *Gott*.

Mamm's face reflected the stress of what was taking place around her. Her tremors were more prominent. Being jostled around in the back of the buggy would not be *gut* for her illness, but their choices were quickly being taken away.

"We must do what is necessary, *dochder*. That man will undoubtedly return with more. I will survive this. The buggy won't be so bad." *Mamm* obviously wanted to put on a brave front, but Willa understood fully how difficult the journey would be on her and the injured marshal.

"I'll take Samantha with me now. Mason will come back for you soon."

Mamm's clear eyes held hers. "I'll only slow you down. You and Mason should take the *kinna* and leave. I'll be *oke* here by myself for a while. What are they going to do with an old woman?"

Willa reached for her mother's hand. "We aren't leaving you. Mason will help you to the buggy as soon as we have Erik inside."

Mamm looked with affection at the sleeping child. "She's a precious one. She told me all about what happened to her *mamm* and *daed*. And about that bear she loves. I hate that she must go through what is she is."

"I do, too." Growing up, Mason used to tease Willa about being the *mamm* of their little group, always worrying over everyone, putting their wishes above hers. Willa had learned it all from her mother's example.

Surviving this man Bartelli was just the beginning. Samantha was all alone in the world and it was heartbreaking to think about what would happen to such an innocent child out in the *Englisch* world.

"Relax for now," she told her mother, and slowly untangled Samantha's tiny arms from around *Mamm*'s waist. "It won't be long before we're ready to move you to the buggy." She gently lifted the child into her arms. The little girl stirred slightly. Her eyes popped open and she stared into Willa's for a moment before she closed them and laid her head against Willa's neck.

Willa sighed gratefully. If the child woke up during the process of moving her to the buggy she'd be frightened. Hopefully, she'd sleep until they were safely away from the house.

"Be careful, *dochder*. I can't lose you, as well."

Willa's hand was suspended over the doorknob. Her mother's tragic words had her turning toward the woman she loved so much.

Though she had no doubt her mother missed both Miriam and her *mann* deeply, she hadn't spoken of the loss in a long time. Sometimes, it was easier just to tuck the grief away and not revisit it.

She turned and smiled. "I miss her, too. And *Daed*. I wish they hadn't left us so soon."

Mamm's expression softened. "*Jah*, but *Gott*'s will must not be questioned no matter how hard it is for us to accept."

Willa thought about the way Miriam had died—taken in a fire set by a man who had become obsessed with her. She'd struggled for a long time to understand how such an act of violence could be *Gott*'s will. How had what happened to Samantha been *Gott*'s will?

Never once had she questioned *Gott*'s sovereignty when it came to the things that happened in this world, or even here in her community, yet she wished she could understand His plan. Why, with everything *Mamm* was going through, had He chosen to take her husband's life? Or her oldest child's?

Willa let go of the momentary doubts. Her faith in *Gott* must be stronger than them. "Don't worry. I'll be careful." Golden Boy noticed her preparing to leave and tried to follow, but she couldn't risk him running outside and being harmed. She gave the command for the dog to stay. Golden Boy grumbled but obeyed.

She forced a smile and left the room. The enormity of what they faced pressed in. It was life and death. Not just hers and Mason's but everyone in this house.

No matter what, she would do everything in her power to prevent her strong mother from having to bury another family member.

Erik stood near the front door, holding on to the frame as if it were the only thing keeping him upright. The strain on his face confirmed how difficult getting upright had been for the injured man. She really hated that they had to force him and her mother into a situation that could turn deadly on a moment's notice.

Mason studied the outside from the living room window. He turned as she approached.

"Do you see anything?" She glanced down at the child, grateful Samantha still slept peacefully.

Mason shook his head and lowered his voice. "Erik has a fever. I'm afraid the wound is on the verge of being infected." He held her gaze. "I sure hope this isn't a mistake." He gently touched the little girl's hair. "I'll take Erik out. You and Samantha stay behind me. Once I get him inside, you and Samantha stay with him while I go back for Beth and Golden Boy."

Willa glanced over to where Erik was barely holding on. "I wish there was some other way, but there isn't." She clasped his arm. "You're making the right decision."

"Thank you," he said, as if the words meant the world to him. "Let's get out of here." He moved to his partner's side and put his arm around Erik's waist. "Keep your eyes open."

With that warning tightening her midsection, Willa followed Mason as he opened the door and assisted Erik out onto the porch. He stopped long enough to scan the woods in front of the house. "I don't see anyone. Are you ready?" He looked over his shoulder at her. Those serious blue eyes pinned hers.

She wasn't, but she would be strong for him. "*Jah*, I'm ready."

They moved forward, Erik stumbling as they crossed the porch. The slightest effort of putting one foot in front of the other came at a cost.

"I got you, brother." Mason held him upright as they reached the steps. Willa kept her arms wrapped tight around the sleeping child.

Step by step Mason somehow managed to get Erik to the buggy. Willa hurried to open the door.

"Here, let me take Samantha from you. I'm going to need your help. Erik, can you hold on to the buggy for a second?"

Erik confirmed. Before she could transfer the child into Mason's arms, Samantha woke up. Her frightened eyes latched on to Willa.

"You're safe," Willa assured her, and did her best to calm the child. "We're going to take a buggy ride."

The child squirmed in her arms, vigorously shaking her head. "I don't want to leave."

Mason took her from Willa. "Samantha, look at me." The child's frantic eyes met his. "Be strong for me. We must leave. It's not safe to stay."

Erik mumbled something.

Willa didn't understand the words. "What did you say?"

Before Erik could repeat it, a sound coming from the other side of the buggy made it clear. "Someone's coming," Willa whispered in a frightened tone.

"We're too late." Mason sat Samantha on the ground and edged to the back of the buggy.

When Samantha would have followed, Willa grabbed her hand and held on to it. "You must stay with me, *kinna*."

A second later, Mason returned. "I counted at least a dozen men. There's probably more." The buggy wouldn't keep them shielded from the front door as they tried to reach the house. "I'll cover you. Can you help Erik inside?"

She would do whatever he needed. "What about you?" How could she leave him here alone with so many?

"Don't worry about me—just get everyone into the house. I'll be right behind you." Mason leaned down to Samantha's level. "Stay in front of Willa and run as fast as you can when she tells you." He straightened. "Hurry, Willa. I can't hold them off for long."

She drew in a shaky breath and nodded.

Mason crept to the back of the buggy. Once in position, he looked over his shoulder, nodded and opened fire.

"Now, Samantha!" With her heart racing, Willa gathered Samantha in front of her and tightened her arm around Erik's waist.

While Mason kept the men pinned back, Willa struggled to get Erik up the steps.

Inside the house, Golden Boy barked ferociously. He must have heard the shots and wanted to come to the rescue. Willa was grateful the door was closed so the dog couldn't get out because she believed he would go after those dangerous men and would probably die for his valor.

Samantha raced across the porch and reached for the door handle. She threw it open and kept right on running.

"Stay, Golden Boy," Willa told the dog before he jutted from the house. She stumbled with Erik over the final step, her breathing labored from the exertion.

With strength she hadn't known she possessed, Willa all but dragged Erik across the porch while Mason continued shooting behind them. Erik's foot hit the threshold. Almost there. Before they could step across into safety, a wave of shots showered down all around them. The men were shooting back.

Willa lost her hold on Erik and both hit the porch. He screamed as Willa covered his body with hers.

"Go, Willa. Get inside the house," she heard Mason yelling.

Golden Boy barked nearby, almost as if he were urging her on.

Willa heard a tiny voice calling for the dog. Samantha. Golden Boy's feet padded across the wood floor in answer.

She had to get Erik inside the house before they took a stray bullet.

"Can you crawl?" she asked against Erik's ear. "We can't stay here. We'll die."

"I think so." Erik managed to get on his hands and knees. Each movement would probably amount to more damage to the marshal's injured body, but he ignored the cost and kept going.

As Erik continued his slow trek, Willa glanced over her shoulder. The men outnumbered Mason, and they knew it. They would come for him soon enough. She couldn't let that happen.

Willa grabbed the handgun from her apron pocket and started shooting. The men stopped their barrage long enough to take cover.

She grabbed Erik around the waist and pulled him the rest of the way inside. He slid to the floor at her feet. Willa turned, expecting to see Mason behind her. He was heading for the stairs when another round of shots forced him back to the buggy.

"Mason!" Terrified he would die, she started after him, but he stopped her.

"No. Go back inside."

She didn't want to leave him, but she had to think about Erik. He remained in the line of fire. Willa closed the door and helped Erik to his feet. She eased him back to the sofa and looked around for Samantha. The little girl huddled behind the sofa, clutching Golden Boy tight.

Willa hit the floor as stray bullets flew through the wooden exterior and lodged into the opposing wall.

She was terrified that, with so much gunfire, Mason would be struck.

"Stay down and where you are," Willa told Erik and Samantha. When a brief reprise occurred, she crawled across the floor to the door. She had to do whatever she could for Mason.

Willa leaned out and aimed at the advancing men. Several cries assured her she'd hit at least some. She ducked out of sight and stayed low when the men swiftly returned fire. Steadying her nerves, she shot again. "Hurry, Mason. They're coming."

He turned at the sound of her voice. "I have to get the horse out of the line of fire before its shot. Stay inside and get down."

Mason moved to the buggy door. Willa continued shooting while she watched in horror as the mare reared up on her hind legs and pawed the air. Mason quickly unwound the reins from the porch before the animal hurt herself.

"Cover me," he yelled.

She fired again. Mason disappeared inside the buggy. He gave the command and the frightened mare shot forward at a frantic speed. Somehow, Mason kept the animal under control. The horse turned around the side of the house and away from danger.

Willa did her best to keep the men pinned down until Mason was out of their firing range. But when a round of bullets strafed the front near the door, she jumped back inside and hit the floor. She reached up and locked the door, then covered her head as more rounds flew around the living room.

The sound of the horse galloping, and the buggy wheels rattling, came from behind the house. Willa kept low and started for the back door, hoping there wouldn't be more shooters in that direction.

Samantha leaped from her hiding spot beside Erik and grabbed for Willa's hand. The dog followed at her heels. With bullets landing all around, Samantha was in danger of being struck.

"*Komm* with me. I will be back for you," Willa told Erik, and hurried Samantha along to her *mamm*'s room and opened the door. The dog passed them and paced the room with a whine. The situation was way beyond anything Golden Boy had experienced.

Mamm sat up as they entered. "What's happening? So many shots."

"I'll explain soon. Mason is in danger." She leaned close to Samantha. "Stay here until I come back."

"No." Samantha's trembling plea tore free. She clung to Willa's hand, tears filling her eyes. "I don't want you to go."

Willa knelt beside the little child. "Mason is out there alone. If I don't let him in, he could die. He wouldn't want me to put you in danger,

Samantha. Please, trust me. Wait here with my mother and Golden Boy. We'll both be back soon."

Samantha's chin wobbled but she slowly nodded.

"Good girl." Willa hugged the child close before she let her go.

With a final look at the woman in the bed, Willa started back for Erik when a sound at the back caught her attention. She moved to the window. The mare rounded the corner of the house, her eyes flashing with fear. The only sound now was the noise made by the horse and buggy. Where had the men gone? She caught sight of Mason pulling back on the reins.

"Whoa, mare," he yelled multiple times before the horse eventually followed his command and came to an ugly stop, snorting and stomping the ground.

Willa ran to the door, unlocked it and threw it open. "Hurry, Mason." As soon as their attackers spotted the buggy, they'd realize Mason hadn't gone far. She couldn't imagine what would happen once they figured out everyone they were looking for could be found hiding inside the house.

Mason swung from the buggy and wrapped

the reins around a porch post before he ran inside. Willa slammed the door shut and locked it.

"They're everywhere. More than I can count." He hurried to the front of the house. At the edge of the window, he kept out of sight as he looked out. "We're trapped, Willa. There's no way we can get out now."

Panic set in at the dreadful truth. "What can we do? There must be something." She wouldn't accept that such bad men were going to win. It wasn't fair for Samantha's story to end here.

Mason's attention returned to the world outside. "Where did they go? They were there a second ago. I don't see anyone."

Willa slipped behind him and looked over his shoulder. Nothing but her quiet homestead appeared in their limited view.

"I don't like it." Mason urged her away from the window. "With all the gunfire, it's possible one of your *Englischer* neighbors would have heard and called the sheriff, but we can't count on that." His hands descended on her shoulders. "No matter what, we can't give up. There's too much at stake." Willa wasn't sure which of them he wanted to convince.

He slipped to the back window. "So far, I don't see anyone back here, but we'll never get everyone into the buggy before they hear us.

They'll shoot us all if we try to leave." He appeared to struggle with a solution. "There's no way I'm leaving you alone to protect two sick people and a child. Not with a virtual army surrounding the house."

The hopelessness in his eyes was hard to witness. No matter what, she wouldn't let him take on the burden alone. "We'll figure it out together. Let's take a moment." She remembered her *mamm* saying that many times growing up. *When things seem impossible, take a step back and talk to* Gott.

She breathed in deep and then noticed blood on his jacket. "You're bleeding again. Were you shot?"

Mason struggled out of his jacket. Blood stained the front of his shirt near his shoulder wound. "It must have reopened."

The sight of the blood brought home how serious their situation truly had become. "Let me check the bandage." She started to examine the wound, but Mason reached for her wrist and stopped her.

"I'm fine." He held her gaze. "We can't count on anyone else coming to our aid. We'll have to do what we can to secure the house and keep them from gaining entrance."

But it would be a temporary solution. Without help, it was only a matter of time before Bartelli's men came for them.

Willa squared her shoulders. Mason and everyone else in the house counted on her to pull her weight, and she wouldn't let any of them down. "What do you need me to do?"

Admiration shone in his eyes. "First thing is to make sure we secure the doors and windows. Do you have a hammer and nails?"

The request took her by surprise. "I think *Daed* kept some in one of the kitchen drawers. I'll get them."

Willa went to the kitchen and rummaged through the drawers until she found a handful of nails and an old hammer, then she went to check on Erik, who leaned against the side of the sofa.

"I'm okay," he murmured when she shook him gently. "Is Mason safe?"

She knelt beside him and felt his forehead. It was cool to the touch. A *gut* thing. "He is. We are securing the doors and windows." She held up the hammer and nails. But they needed to get Erik to a safer spot.

"Don't worry about me," he said as if reading her thoughts. "I'm fine here for now. Get the house secured before they try to break in."

She squeezed his arm. "We will. And then we will come get you."

Willa left him for the moment and returned to Mason. She told him about Erik.

"He's safe for now, but I'd prefer to have him with Beth and Samantha. As soon as we have the back entry secured, I'll get him." Mason moved to the door. He turned with a thoughtful look on his face.

"What are you thinking?" she asked.

"You said you know your neighbor behind you fairly well?"

She had no idea where he was going with this. "That's right. Mr. Connors comes by and checks on us from time to time. He's a *gut* man."

"Is he familiar with your animals? Would he know the mare belonged here should the animal happen on his property?"

The truth dawned quickly. "*Jah*, I believe so." Hope began to take hold.

"It's something. Regardless, we can't leave the animal attached to the buggy. It could get shot. I'm going to free her. Hopefully, she'll head away from the house where all the gunshots are and toward Connors's place."

But if Mason went outside again… "It's too dangerous." Willa sat the hammer and nails down and moved closer. "You could die."

"I don't have a choice. It's a long shot that may not work, but I have to do something."

He held her gaze. "If we don't do it, everyone will die."

The truth struck like a blow. They were all out of options.

He returned to the window and parted the curtains. "There's no one back there," he said in a bewildered tone. "Kind of strange since they had to see the direction I went. I'm surprised they haven't kicked in the door by now." He frowned as he surveyed the backyard. "Stand guard at the door."

She slowly nodded. Mason checked the window one final time. "I don't see anyone, but they could be hiding in the woods." Willa picked up on his unease. Would he be walking into a setup?

He moved to the door with her. "Stay out of sight as best you can." His gaze held hers for a long moment. "We're running low on bullets. Only shoot if you have a clear shot of hitting someone."

Mason unlocked the door and slowly opened it. She couldn't imagine how much courage it took to step outside.

Willa kept the door cracked enough to see the back of the house. The family's old smokehouse was in her line of sight between the house and the woods. *Mamm*'s chicken coop wasn't far from it with all her little feathered friends inside.

Mason ducked down low and eased himself across the porch to the buggy without opposition. He slowly moved to the front where the mare stood with her ears at alert and eyes wild.

The slightest of movement in the woods to the left of the house grabbed her attention.

"Mason, to your left." A glint warned her that their attackers had expected this move and were ready for it. Willa pointed the weapon toward the glint and fired. Metal tinged off metal. A scream followed. She tucked behind the door but kept her eyes on the woods.

Mason worked quickly to release the horse. He slapped its flank hard. The animal whinnied fearfully and thundered off behind the house away from the danger. And in the direction of Ethan Connors's place. Willa prayed the animal wouldn't stop before it reached her neighbor's ranch.

A second man appeared at the tree line and began shooting in Willa's direction. She stooped. Several shots lodged into the door frame where she'd stood moments earlier. Mason. He was still out there. Every second meant danger and possible death.

When the shooting lulled, Willa carefully peered past the door. Mason hunkered down near the wheel of the buggy. Her vision darted from him to the woods once more. Where had the second shooter gone?

Mason spotted her standing there and waved her back inside. Willa ignored his concern and focused on the woods. The shooter reappeared with another man. They stepped into the opening, their weapons drawn and ready. Mason wouldn't stand a chance against so many.

Willa shot again, and they retreated. She ran for Mason. "Hurry." Her hand circled his arm. They just had time to make it through the door when an all-too-familiar sound of gunshots erupted. A round of bullets flew through the house jamming into walls. She and Mason hit the floor. Mason scrambled over to the door and relocked it.

He gathered her close and moved away from the danger zone. "I don't think that lock will hold up should they try to break in. We need something heavy to put against the door to help secure it." Mason shook his head. "They're waiting for someone. That's the only explanation for why they haven't already stormed the house."

Willa struggled to think of something they could use. Her *mamm*'s dresser would work for the back door. She'd have to find something else for the front entrance.

A noise nearby had them both whirling toward it. Samantha slipped from *Mamm*'s room, her tiny face distorted with fear. She spotted Mason and ran into his arms. "I'm scared, Mr. Mason."

"Oh, honey." Mason scooped her up despite the strain on his reopened wound. He held the frightened child while she hid her face against his chest.

"*Mamm* has a heavy dresser in her room. We could pull it against the door." Would it be enough to keep so many from breaking in?

"That will work. Help me get it to the back door. We'll have to find something else to block the front."

Willa went to speak to *Mamm* along with Mason, who cradled Samantha close. Golden Boy, in a perpetual state of agitation, stood at the foot of the bed with his hackles up, a low whine coming from his throat.

Her mother's fearful expression darted between them. "Those shots came from the back of the house. Are we surrounded?"

"There are a lot of men," Mason told her, and explained about the horse.

"Do you think Ethan will come to our aid?"

Willa turned to Mason. He appeared to be weighing his answer. "There's a slim chance, but I'm worried he will be walking into an ambush if he does. He could be killed."

Willa shivered. "I know he was once in the military, but still, this is not something he would be expecting."

Mason carried Samantha to *Mamm*'s bed. "Can you be strong for me?"

Her huge tearful eyes held his. She slowly nodded. "Stay here with Beth and Golden Boy while Willa and I secure the doors and windows."

Samantha wiped her eyes. "O-kay."

Mason smiled at the child's bravery. "Good girl. I'll be right back as soon as we've finished securing the house."

Samantha scooched close to *Mamm*, watching them move the dresser.

As soon as they'd gotten the object from the room, Willa closed the door. The less her mother and Samantha witnessed of what happened outside the walls of the bedroom, the better.

Working together, they pushed and pulled the dresser over to the back door and shoved it as close as they could possibly get it.

"That should at least provide some resistance." He straightened and surveyed the blocked entrance. "Let's get Erik back to

Beth's room, and then we'll secure the front door and fortify the windows."

Mason headed into the living room and to his partner.

With Willa's help, they got Erik to his feet. "We're moving you to a safer place," he told Erik.

Moving slowly, they reached Beth's room and all but carried Erik over to the rocker in the corner.

With Erik settled, Mason went over to *Mamm*'s bed. "I'm sorry about this, Beth. I know this is the last thing you need to be dealing with."

Mamm never hesitated in speaking her mind. "No matter what happens here, you are an honorable man, and you are doing what *Gott* wishes you to do to protect this precious *kinna*. And us."

Yet with a virtual army of bad men gunning for them, and no one coming to their aide, Willa couldn't imagine the pressure resting on Mason's shoulders.

When the sun set on this day, she wondered if any of them would be alive to tell the truth about what really happened here today.

EIGHT

Doing what God wished? Beth's sentiments burrowed deep down into his heart like a bullet, and they felt just as dangerous. Like a physical blow. If anyone didn't deserve to be called an instrument of God, it was him. He'd made so many wrong moves in life. Hurt people close to him. Why would God choose to use him?

The woman slowly wasting away in her bed had more faith than he'd had in a long time. The realization embarrassed him. At one point, God had held a treasured part of his heart.

He forced a smile and squeezed Beth's hand before turning his attention to Samantha. "Try not to worry. We're safe." He didn't know for certain, but this little girl shouldn't have to hear his doubts. He had to be strong for her where others had failed.

Samantha's frightened eyes clung to his. She'd lived through so many bad things. She deserved to have nothing but happiness from here on out.

The child hugged him tight with those little arms while her body trembled. He'd asked her to be strong for him many times in the past. When did she get to be just a normal little girl again?

Over the top of Samantha's head, Mason sought out Willa. She would stand beside him and do whatever he asked her to because she trusted him.

"We need to get the front door secured before they breach it."

You are doing what Gott *wishes you to do to protect this precious* kinna.

Beth's words wouldn't go away. He swallowed several times, trying to fight past feelings of inadequacy. He'd failed so many people in the past. Would this be yet another example of his unworthiness with a high price tag attached to it?

Mason held Samantha tight and did something he hadn't done since he was a young man living here.

Help me. The words slipped out, unfamiliar like a foreign language. He waited, unsure of what he expected. Maybe the ceiling to fly away and the skies to part. God's voice to assure him everything would work out. None of those things happened and he forced down his regret and slowly untangled Samantha's little arms from his neck. "Be strong for me."

Samantha's solemn eyes appeared so grown up. "I will try, Mr. Mason."

The trust on her sweet face strengthened his resolve. They might be outnumbered by Bartelli's men with no means of reaching out to anyone, but he was a trained marshal. He wouldn't let Bartelli hurt this little girl or anyone else in this house.

He was so proud of Samantha. "That's my girl." He nodded to Willa and they stepped out of the room. Mason quietly closed the door with hands that shook. The stakes were so high.

"We can use *Mamm*'s hutch in the kitchen to secure the front door."

Mason smiled down at her and touched her face. "That should work." Though he didn't say as much, Mason was sure she understood that everything they were doing at this point would provide little resistance against Bartelli's determined men.

With her at his side, he went to the kitchen.

"Do you remember when your *daed* made the hutch for my mother?"

He did. "Absolutely. Fletcher and I helped my father bring it over on the wagon. I remember Beth was pleased to get it set up in the kitchen."

"Yes, she was."

Beth had loved the piece so much. She hadn't stopped thanking Mason's father for making it. As one of the few things Beth had that she treasured, he hated using it with the realization it would probably get shot up, but if it meant the difference between saving lives or not, there was no question what Beth would want him to do.

"I'll empty it first." Willa removed the dishes Beth kept inside while Mason gave her a hand.

Once they'd finished, they worked together to move the hutch into the living room and against the door. Would it be strong enough to withstand the storm coming their way? He sure hoped so.

"What do we do now?"

Mason looked at her pretty face and wished he had a good answer for her. They'd done everything possible to secure the doors. "We nail the windows shut and wait and pray someone—perhaps your neighbor—has heard the gunshots and called the sheriff."

The disappointment on her face confirmed

this was not the answer she'd hoped for. But he couldn't make her promises that might not happen.

With Willa's help, he finished securing the rest of the windows in the house.

"That is the last one," Willa said once they'd finished with the window over the kitchen sink.

Too restless to sit around and wait for what was coming next, Mason went to the back of the house and checked the backyard. The horseless buggy obscured part of his view. He moved to another window that afforded a different vantage point. From here, the smokehouse and the chicken coop blocked part of the woods from sight. Where had the shooters gone? What were they waiting for?

His mind went back to why the men were basically standing down. "I don't understand it. They have us on our heels. Why not storm the house?" He blew out a sigh. "I'm glad they haven't, though. We're low on ammo." Yet he had to believe they were waiting for someone. He turned to Willa as frustration took hold. It was the only explanation. Bartelli wasn't one to hesitate. His people had come here for a purpose.

She came to the same conclusion as he did.

"You think they are waiting for something to happen?"

Mason latched on to her face. "More likely, *someone* to arrive." From the scant information they'd been able to obtain on how Bartelli handled most of his hits, other than the way things had gone down with Samantha's parents, the man always had his second-in-command handle his dirty work.

To this date, no one had been able to get close enough to the organization and live to tell anything about this man.

"I think they're waiting for Bartelli's second-in-command," Mason told her. If Bartelli's people were awaiting Ombra's arrival, things were about to get really bad. Rumor had it, the man's penchant for torture made Bartelli look like a choirboy.

Willa's eyes reflected fear. "I can't believe you have no idea who this man is."

He scrubbed a hand across weary eyes. "The commands filter down the ranks from Bartelli to Ombra, and then to a series of mid-level lieutenants before they reach Bartelli's men on the streets who work with the gangs to arrange gun sales. The only way we were able to originally tie the weapons to Bartelli was through the ship manifesto that brought them into the country. It was registered under Lucian's name."

Willa visibly shuddered. "Such evil is terrifying."

Mason reached for her hand. "Yes, it is. The deeper I dig into Bartelli's history, the more I'm reminded how far removed that way of life is from the Amish faith. That such different spectrums of good and bad can exist in the world is mind-boggling. It reminds me how much I've missed this simple world."

She smiled gently. "You're missed here, as well. By your family. Your *bruders*. Eli. Your *mamm*."

Eli missed him? Impossible after all the turmoil he'd caused by accusing Eli of stealing Miriam's affections away. Instead of staying and accepting the truth—and realizing his anger with his brother was the result of something much deeper—he'd left his family and God. How could he expect forgiveness?

He stuffed the bad down deep. He'd gotten good at that, and there were far worse things coming their way—especially if Ombra had any part in them.

"Let's look in on Erik and see how he's holding up. I'd like to check on Beth and Samantha, too. Then, for my own peace of mind, let's double-check all the entry points." Because the waiting was the hardest. He glanced Willa's way. She smiled sadly.

He let her hand go and went to Beth's room where Erik didn't appear to have moved. Mason hurried to his partner's side and checked and found a faint pulse. A helpless feeling settled over him. He couldn't imagine losing his partner to Bartelli's evil plots. Erik's family didn't deserve any of this.

He thought about Donna—Erik's wife. She'd made Mason promise every time they began a new case to watch out for her husband. Donna knew the risks, especially with this case. But he'd promised, anyway, and he wouldn't let Donna down.

Willa touched Erik's forehead. "At least the fever appears to have broken. That's something."

Mason checked the wound. It was bleeding again. The exertion from earlier had reopened it.

"Stay with him," he told Willa. "I'll get the necessary supplies and be right back." Mason went to the kitchen and grabbed what he needed then returned to his injured partner.

With Willa's assistance, they packed the wound and rebandaged it.

"That should hold up," Mason told him.

"Thank you, brother," Erik managed, and

leaned back against the chair and closed his eyes. Watching his partner look so weak was terrifying.

"It appears the medicine is working. That is *gut* news."

He held on to what Willa said because he needed something positive and did his best not to show the consuming fear.

"I will be right back. I'm going to check the front of the house." He slipped from the room before she could respond. Reaching the living room window, Mason noticed the rain had slowed to a gentle drizzle, but low-hanging clouds isolated the farm from the rest of the world. Without any confirmation they would be rescued, Mason was all out of options. And he bared his heart to God.

Lord, I don't know what to do. These are people whose lives are threatened. There is so much darkness surrounding us. But I remember Your light shines the brightest in the darkness. Shine Your light on this situation and show me what to do. I confess, I've turned my back on You, but I know You were always there waiting for me. Help me, Lord. Help me save these people.

Tears choked him up. The prayer left him broken and feeling undeserving of God's redemption. Mason swallowed several times and turned to find Willa standing beside him.

"He has everything under His control," she said softly. "We have to trust Him."

Could he have that much faith in light of what was coming?

He gently placed his hands on her shoulders and looked into her eyes. "One way or another, whether they're waiting for Ombra or not, it's only a matter of time before they try to break into the house."

She never looked away. "I know. But we have something they don't. We have *Gott*."

He so wanted to believe her. Because with no means of reaching out to anyone, he and Willa would be forced to fight off a group of men who were determined their story would end here. In this house.

She understood what he didn't want to tell her. Their chances of surviving the almost certain attack were slim.

Willa fought not to lose the small amount of hope she still possessed. She couldn't believe *Gott* would choose this ending for Samantha or any of them. They had to keep trying.

Staying busy helped take her mind off what was coming. She'd weathered the loss of Miriam and her *daed*, as well as Mason's leaving the community, by not letting her hands remain idle. Willa couldn't sit around and wait for an attack she felt ill-equipped to survive. "There must be something more we can do."

He came over to where she stood and put his arm around her shoulders. "I'll think of something."

Willa slipped her arm around his waist and smiled. She'd heard him say those same words many times growing up. Usually when they were about to get into trouble for something they weren't supposed to do. "You were always trying to fix things. Even when they weren't fixable."

He looked into her eyes and she stopped smiling. "Sometimes things are damaged beyond fixing," he murmured, and she wondered if he was talking about himself or his faith.

Willa touched his cheek. "I don't believe that. There is always a way. Sometimes it may not be clear, but if you look, you'll find it."

He shifted her to face him and clasped her hand in his. "I wish I had your faith."

The depth of hurt she saw in him was hard to witness. "You can. Ask *Gott* to help you." She hesitated. "Mason, if you are unhappy with your life you can change it. As long as you have breath in here." She touched his chest. "Change is possible."

His laugh held bitterness. "My family. I've hurt them and yours. I wasn't here when my father passed away. Or my grandfather and so many others. And I wasn't there for my family during those times. All they remember is that angry boy who ran away because he didn't get what he wanted. Because Miriam chose my brother instead of me."

Willa wouldn't let him continue to believe this. "You are wrong. Your family remembers the *bruder* and *sohn* they love. The one they wish to be reunited with." She looked into his eyes and told him what she believed in her heart. "And I don't think you left West Kootenai simply because you lost Miriam to Eli."

He shifted without saying a word.

"You left because of Chandler. You were in pain and you didn't understand how to deal with all that hurt."

He hung his head.

"Chandler's death wasn't your fault," she insisted. "You have to stop blaming yourself."

He let her go and stepped back. "It was my fault, Willa," he muttered. "I was older than Chandler by a year. He looked up to me. I should have protected him. Instead, I got him killed."

"You didn't. You had no way of knowing the ice would be so thin on the lake. All the *kinner* skated there. Miriam and I had just a few days before the accident." She clutched his arms. "It was a tragic accident—nothing more."

But he didn't believe her.

"Oh, Mason." She tugged him into her arms and held him. "Ask *Gott* to free you of this guilt. He wouldn't want you to carry it a day longer. Let Him set you free so you can live your life the way He wants you to."

He clutched her tighter and released a heavy sigh that seemed to come from his soul. "I want that. I want to make things right with my family. With God. I'm so tired of carrying this guilt around."

She leaned back and smiled up at him. "Then don't. It's not yours to carry."

He smiled genuinely and kissed her forehead. "You always were such a wise one." As he continued to look at her, his smile slowly disappeared. "I really missed you," he whispered.

Her heart kicked out a strange rhythm. As a young girl, she'd once longed for him to look at her like this. She had been in love with Mason Shetler since she was old enough to understand what love meant—even through that brief time when he imagined himself in love with Miriam.

But her love would never be. As much as

it broke her heart, if they survived this nightmare, her future would not be with Mason. Even if he chose to return to West Kootenai and the Amish way. Mason deserved to be with someone who could give him children. A future. Years of happiness together. But the life Mason so longed for would not come from her. How could she open her heart to him when the future waiting for her was almost certainly filled with darkness and death?

NINE

The quiet at the back of the house was the most disturbing. Mason's nerves were on edge. An eerie calm settled around them and all he could think about was the nightmare of danger coming their way.

Willa brought over a cup of coffee and handed it to him. "Anything?"

He shook his head and accepted the coffee. "Nothing. I don't even see the men anymore. How's Erik?"

"He's resting, but the wound is getting worse and his fever has returned. I gave him some antibiotics that I had." She held his gaze and shrugged.

The knot in his stomach tightened at what she wasn't saying. Mason surveyed the space behind the house from the window.

He rubbed his tired eyes and sipped the strong coffee, hoping it would clear away the exhaustion enough to keep him alert.

"Do you think Peppermint made it to Ethan's ranch?" Willa's full attention stayed on his face.

Chances are the horse would have kept on the path she had started down, which would lead her to the ranch in question, but it wasn't a given. "I'd say it's a good possibility." He kept his misgivings to himself because he didn't want her to lose hope.

He squeezed her arm. "I'm going to check in on Samantha and your mom. Should we bring Beth some of this delicious coffee?"

Willa's smile didn't diminish the worry on her face. "I'll get her some. You go ahead." She started for the kitchen. Even with only a couple of steps separating them, her soft footsteps were drowned out by the sudden noise of a dozen or more weapons being fired at the front of the house. Shots ripped through the windowpanes and sent shards of glass and bullets flying all around.

"Get down!" Mason yelled, and dropped the coffee cup as he hit the floor at the same time additional shots sprayed across the back.

Scrambling across the floor, he reached Willa and pulled her inside Beth's room. "We need to get everyone on the ground." Golden Boy barked several times as Mason crawled over to his partner and lowered him to the floor while Willa grabbed Samantha and held her close.

"Sit, Golden Boy," Willa told the dog.

Mason kept as low as possible and moved to Beth's side. "I'm going to get you down to the floor. It will be safer there."

The shooting abruptly stopped. An unnerving silence followed.

He quickly gathered Beth, along with her quilt, in his arms and placed her on the floor beside Willa.

The brief reprieve was broken by more gunshots. Samantha covered her ears and buried her face against Willa.

"As soon as we get another break, we'll move all of you down to the cellar," Mason told them. "It's the safest room. There aren't any windows, and if we cover up the entrance, Bartelli's people won't know the room is there."

Willa didn't take her eyes off him. She would understand if that happened, the chances of the two of them surviving were slim.

Willa held Samantha close. "We are *oke*, *kinna*. We are all *oke*."

Mason moved to Willa's side and stroked the child's hair. "I know it's scary, Samantha, but you are doing great."

The little girl rubbed her hand over her face and turned teary eyes his way. "Why do they want to hurt us, Mr. Mason? Why did Uncle Lucian hurt my daddy and mommy?"

How did he explain the darkness that existed in the world to this guiltless child? "He's a bad man, kiddo." His jaw tightened when he thought about what Samantha had gone through. To protect Samantha, he'd fight to the death every last one of the men Bartelli sent their way.

She slowly nodded. "Promise you won't let him hurt me. Promise you and Mr. Erik won't die."

He didn't hesitate. "I promise." The weight of his promise settled over him as he moved to the door. Several sporadic shots sounded in both directions.

"I'll be right back." He stepped out into the hall. The living room looked like someone had set off a bomb inside it. The back of the house had taken less damage.

Mason slipped past the damaged living room to the kitchen. He quickly moved the rug and opened the trapdoor.

Before he headed back to the others, he had to get something off his chest. He wanted to have his faith restored, and yet nothing about what was happening to them brought it back. In fact, he felt tested beyond what he could endure.

"Lord, if You want me to believe in You

again, trust You, then You'd better help me save them. I may not be deserving of saving, but they didn't ask for any of this." The words slipped out. He collected himself and rubbed a hand across the tears in his eyes. "Please— save them."

Silence was his only answer. He waited a minute longer, not sure really what he expected to happen. Maybe some Godly wisdom that would save the day?

He shook his head. If they were going to be saved, it was up to him to figure out how.

Mason returned to Beth's room. "It's quiet. Maybe they're reloading or maybe…" He caught himself before he said *preparing to storm the house*. "Anyway, this is our chance to get everyone into the cellar." He drew in air and went over to his partner. "Are you ready?"

Erik looked up at him, eyes filled with exhaustion that went much deeper than physical, yet he never wavered, as he hadn't since they'd first become partners. "I'm ready."

Assisting him to his feet, Mason kept a tight hold as they slowly headed for the door. "Bring Samantha," he tossed over his shoulder. "Beth, I'll be right back for you."

Beth possessed a bravery that couldn't be faked. "Go. Take care of your friend."

"I will, but I'm coming back for you," he insisted, and he would. No matter what.

Reaching the door proved excruciatingly slow. Erik could barely keep his feet under him; the full weight of his lanky frame almost took Mason down.

He slowly opened the door and stepped out into the hall. The quiet around them was far from comforting. Mason glanced behind him to assure Willa had followed. She held Samantha in her arms while the dog kept at her side.

Golden Boy trotted down the stairs ahead of them.

"Take Samantha down first," he told Willa. "I'll need your support with Erik."

She sat Samantha on her feet and grabbed the lantern from the table. "Stay close to me." Willa headed down the steps with the little girl clutching her arm.

Once they reached the cellar, Willa said, "I'm going to help Mr. Mason. Stay here with Golden Boy."

Mason didn't hear the child's answer, but a few seconds later Willa stood beside him.

"I'll go first. Erik, can you hold on to me?"

Erik murmured something unintelligible but grabbed hold of Mason's shoulder.

"Willa, do what you can to help him stay upright." She answered with a nod.

It took both of them to get Erik down to the cellar. A single chair and a cot were the only furniture in the place. He lowered his partner onto the cot. The room had to be ten degrees colder than the top floor.

"I'll get some quilts," Willa said as she disappeared up the stairs. She came back with an armful of quilts and a pillow. Carefully, she placed the pillow under Erik's head while Mason covered his shivering friend with a quilt.

"I'm going back for Beth." Erik didn't respond. His condition had deteriorated quickly and there was nothing Mason could do to save Erik but make him as comfortable as possible.

"I'll come with you." Willa knelt in front of Samantha. "Can you take care of Erik and Golden Boy while Mason and I bring down my mother?"

"No," the little girl sobbed and clung to her hand.

Willa knelt beside her. "How about we play a game. Can you count to one hundred?"

Samantha's frightened eyes held hers. "Y-yes."

Willa smiled. "*Gut.* Count slowly to one hundred for me. Mr. Mason and I will be back before you finish."

The dog moved to Samantha's side as if understanding the child needed comfort. The little girl wrapped her arms around Golden Boy's neck and started counting. "One. Two."

Willa squeezed the child's shoulder. "You are doing great." She rose and followed Mason.

Upstairs, he moved to the shattered window. Keeping out of sight, he looked out between the billowing curtains. What he saw didn't make sense. "It's as if they've fallen back for some reason." Not for a moment did he believe Bartelli's men had simply left. He had a bad feeling they wouldn't have the luxury of this peace for long. Mason stepped into Beth's room with Willa.

"I don't hear anything. What's happening?" Beth's worried gaze grabbed hold of him.

"They're preparing for something. Let's get you to the cellar before they make their move." Mason moved to the bed. "Beth, I'm going to be as gentle as possible."

"Do what you have to do." The Beth-like comment had him smiling. He carefully put his arm around her and tried not to react to how fragile she felt, as if her earthly shell were wasting away around her.

They neared the cellar entrance. Mason heard Samantha's soft voice counting. "Forty-one, forty-two."

He slowly descended the steps and deposited Beth onto the chair. "Are you comfortable enough there?" He thought about gathering some blankets from the bed and bringing them down for her to lay on.

"This will suit me fine. And I'm close to Erik and this darling *kinna*."

"Here, *Mamm*." Willa spread one of the quilts over her mother's lap. "Warm enough?"

"*Jah*, I am *gut*." She dismissed Willa's concern and looked up at Mason. "What will you do next?"

He had no idea, but if he didn't come up with something soon, it would mean certain death for all of them. "I'll try the phone again. You never know. The weather has lifted some." Mason handed Erik his service weapon. "Just in case." Erik of all people would understand.

Willa brought down another quilt for Samantha and wrapped it around the little girl's shoulders. "To keep you warm."

Mason hesitated before returning upstairs. He didn't like the way Erik held his side. So far there wasn't any fresh blood on his shirt— a good sign the wound had stopped bleeding. Still, he couldn't help but worry.

He knelt beside Erik and checked the bandage, happy to see a dry covering. "It's looking better," he assured his friend. "Hang on, brother. Just hang on."

Erik grabbed his arm then smiled, and some of Mason's uneasiness disappeared.

Willa left the lantern beside her mother and climbed the stairs after him.

They stood in the kitchen staring at each other.

"What do we do now?" Willa asked.

He pulled out the phone once more in a desperate attempt. The signal was nonexistent. With a frustrated sigh, Mason shoved it back into his pocket. "I was hoping with the storm easing we'd be able to pick up service."

"What will we do if they try to break into the house next?"

"We keep fighting." He exhaled the words. "We do everything we can to stay alive until somebody reports all this shooting. By now, someone has to have noticed." He sure hoped this proved true.

He tugged her into his arms. "I know this is hard. I'm so sorry, Willa."

She leaned back and looked at him, her green eyes filled with strength. "*Nay*, there's nothing to apologize for. This isn't your fault."

But he believed differently. He'd brought these dangerous men to her and Beth when Beth wasn't able to fight back.

She cupped his face with her hands. "Mason, you always took on blame that wasn't yours. You feel deeply, and I admire this greatly about you, but what is happening here isn't your fault. You're doing everything you can to save that child. Everything."

The words humbled him. "I'm the one who admires you. Even as a little girl you were courageous. Josiah and Miriam would be proud of you, just as Beth is."

Her eyes widened. Before he could say what was in his heart, a board creaked near the front door. "Someone's on the porch." The whispered words filled the space between them. "Stay here."

Mason slipped over to where he could see the door properly. Wind drove the light rain inside the broken window, soaking the floor where he stood. Two men stood beside the door. They were going to try to break in. Mason fired at one of the suspects through the broken glass. The man grabbed his leg and fell to the porch. The second man reached for his partner and hauled him up. They stumbled from the porch and ran for the woods.

Shooting came from the woods near where the two men had disappeared. "Stay down." Mason ran toward the kitchen as bullets flew through the walls and all around them...then silence.

Willa moved to his side. "What are they doing?"

Mason believed he knew. "My guess? If

Ombra is the one calling the shots, he's waiting for darkness before mounting an all-out attack. Right now, they can't be sure how many armed people are inside the house. He's doing enough to keep us on our toes. We won't be able to see their approach at night." He turned to her. "Regardless, we need a plan B."

All her doubts were there for him to see. He was desperate enough to take out the phone and hold it up to the lantern light. He almost dropped it when he noticed the signal indicator registered a single bar. "There's service." He dialed 9-1-1 and listened. The call didn't go through.

Disappointment hit him like a blow. Keeping his reaction to himself was impossible. "I don't know what to do next. It'll be dark in a few hours. We're surrounded. You and I won't be able to hold them off once they storm the house."

She reached for his hands, bowed her head and prayed.

To have such faith must be a comfort. He closed his eyes and waited until she murmured, "Amen."

He'd gotten so many things wrong in his youth. With twenty-twenty hindsight vision Mason saw with clarity what he could not at seventeen. Through the years of beating himself up for the decisions he'd made back then, Mason hadn't really thought about God directing each one of them, taking Mason's missteps and using them for His purposes.

As he looked at Willa's pretty face, the past and the things pulling him away from his home faded. She helped him see that his life wasn't defined by the things he'd done. Despite the circumstances facing them, his heart swelled. Willa showed him the way back to God and for that he would always be grateful.

He brought her hands to his lips and kissed her knuckles. She had endured more than her share of heartache and yet her faith in God never wavered. "I'm so sorry for everything you have gone through. Your family has suffered enough," he said softly.

She steadied herself. "Life is filled with losses. Losing Miriam just about destroyed *Mamm*. And then we lost *Daed*."

"And Beth's illness. That can't be easy for her or you."

She swallowed several times. "It isn't. I don't want to lose my mother." Her voice came out a hoarse whisper.

He gathered her close and rested his head against hers. "I don't want that, either."

She sighed deeply and pulled away. "I guess we both have struggles."

But his were all self-inflicted. As he looked into her eyes, something important became apparent. He'd missed what had been right there before him all those years ago. Willa. She was the one he'd come to for comfort after Chandler's death. The one he shared his dreams for the future with. The one he'd missed through the years.

Why hadn't he seen the truth all along? Was it too late? It tore him apart to think after all these years the life God wanted for him might never be.

Above all else, Mason would always be her friend. Yet when he looked at her like he did right now, it hurt so much. The tenderness she saw in him, the caring, could never be hers.

Mason shifted slightly and placed his hands on her waist, drawing her closer. The expression on his face was all her young heart had wished for at one time. A whisper of air separated them. She searched his face, wondering if she was imagining this moment happening between them. Was she letting the past and her feelings for Mason create something that wasn't there?

She wanted so much to kiss him. To have the right to call him hers, but that would never be. Willa placed her hands over his and then pulled them away. She stepped back, fighting hard to remain strong.

A bleakness replaced the gentleness on his face. He turned away, running a hand across his neck. "I'm going to check the back of the house," he murmured, and started that way without waiting for her to answer.

Willa couldn't even begin to respond. She stood where he'd left her and wondered how much more she would be forced to endure.

"Mr. Mason, come quick! Something's wrong with Mr. Erik." The child's scared voice broke through the misery flooding Willa's heart.

Mason ran past her to the kitchen. He quickly started down the steps as fast as possible. Willa hurried after him.

Samantha ran up to Mason, her tiny face consumed with panic. "I can't wake up Mr. Erik."

Mason moved to his partner's side and felt for a pulse at the base of his neck. "He's alive." He turned to Willa. His ashen face was a reminder of the clock ticking away, marking their impending fate. He gently shook Erik enough to wake him. "Hey there, partner. How are you holding up?"

Erik's eyes fluttered and his answer was muddled.

Mason collected himself before turning to

Samantha. "He's all right, sweetheart, but he's sleepy because of his injury."

Samantha grabbed hold of him. "I'm scared. He wouldn't wake up."

Mason wrapped his arms around the child. Over the top of her head he sought out Willa. "I know you are, sweetie. I am, too. You are being so brave. I'm proud of you. Can you keep being strong for me for a little while longer?"

The little girl nodded. "Y-yes."

He smiled and wiped away her tears. With the child clutching his side, Mason knelt beside Willa's mother. "How are you holding up?"

The tremors had visibly worsened with the stress of what was happening around her. Willa secured the blanket tight around *Mamm*'s frail body and wished there was more she could do.

"Don't worry so," her mother said, and clutched her hand. "I am holding up *gut*."

Willa leaned over to kiss her mother's forehead, then smiled.

"Were you able to get the phone to work?" *Mamm*'s keen eyes held Mason's.

He shook his head. "The phone service here is nonexistent." They had exhausted every possible means available to them. If Ethan or one of the other neighbors didn't call the sheriff to report the gunshots, it was only a matter of time.

"I am praying for us, Mason. *Gott* will show you the way. I'm sure of it. Be careful. Take care of Willa. She's all I have left in this world."

Mason's attention returned to Willa. The same look she'd seen before made her wish for things that were not hers.

"I promise I will," he said softly without looking away.

"I'm thirsty, Mr. Mason. Can I come with you to get some water?" The little girl's request drew his attention away and Willa exhaled.

Mason clasped Samantha's hand in his. "Of course. In fact, we should bring down water and something to eat for everyone," he said quietly, his attention returning to Willa.

They were facing a life-and-death situation. There were other things besides her foolish youthful dreams to think about. She let go of the hurt and nodded. "I will find something," she managed, and climbed the steps behind Mason and Samantha.

"I'll get you some water." Willa went to the sink to fill a glass for Samantha. She turned to hand it to the child, but a whooshing sound grabbed her attention. The glass slipped from her hand and shattered in the sink. Willa spun toward the horrible sound coming from the living room.

"Stay with Samantha." Mason didn't wait for her response. He ran toward the noise.

"Mason, no," she said fearfully, but her warning went unheeded. With Samantha hugging her side, Willa peeked into the living room. The curtains covering the shattered window had caught fire. Something that appeared to be liquid covered the floor and was now catching fire. It spread across the floor.

Horrified, Willa tugged Samantha farther into the kitchen and away from the danger. "Get down on the floor and don't move." The girl's huge eyes were fearful, but she dropped down and curled into a tiny ball.

Willa filled a pitcher with water and tossed it on the flames. "Get a quilt," Mason yelled while stomping at the flames. Smoke filled the room, making it hard to breathe freely. Her eyes filled with tears. They streamed down her face as she edged past the fire to the chest that held several additional quilts she and *Mamm* had completed before her mother's hands became too unsteady.

She grabbed the first one and tossed it to Mason, then brought out a second to help him beat out the flames.

Working together, they managed to get the last of the fire put out. Willa couldn't believe what had happened.

"That was close." Mason wiped soot from his face. "I'm sorry about ruining your handiwork." He tossed the singed quilts aside.

They were the last thing on her mind. She'd tried so hard to remain positive, wanting to believe someone would come to their aid, yet, after everything, her faith was running thin.

She clutched his arm and fought back tears. "Mason, what are we going to do?"

He pulled her to him and held her without saying a word. She couldn't stop the sob that escaped as she listened to his frantic heartbeat and wondered how much more they could take.

Neither noticed Samantha had left the kitchen until she screamed. Mason jerked toward the sound. Samantha stood near the singed curtains.

"Samantha, no!" The child didn't respond, so Mason hurried to her. She appeared to be fixated on something outside.

He tugged her away from danger.

Samantha buried her face against his side. "He's out there."

Mason whirled toward Willa, the confusion on his face matching hers. "Who's out there?" He led both Samantha and Willa from the living room.

"The man who held Mommy," she sobbed.

Mason stopped walking. "The man who held

your mother is out there? You saw the man who held your mother while Lucian shot your father? He's out there now?"

The child's head bobbed up and down. "I saw him. He looks like he did that day." Tears flowed from her eyes.

"What do you mean, he looks like he did then?"

"He's wearing a suit. He held my mother so she couldn't get away." Mason gathered Samantha close while she cried.

"Let's get her back to the cellar," he told Willa. While Mason carried the crying child downstairs, Willa poured water into another pitcher, then gathered glasses and as many packages of crackers and peanut butter as she could carry in her apron.

"She's never been able to identify the man before. This is big," he said as Willa joined them. "Can you stay here with Samantha? I'm going to cover the window so they can't see into the house."

As much as she wanted to stay down here where it was safe, Mason needed her. "Let me help," Willa said. "I'm not leaving you to handle what's happening up there alone."

He immediately rejected the idea. "It's too dangerous. If something happens to you…"

She reached for his hand. "I will be fine. I

know you hate putting me in the line of fire, but we're fighting an innumerable army that's steadily increasing their attacks. It's way beyond one man's capability. Let me help you."

"All right," he said at last, but she could see how hard it was to say those words. Mason left the cellar. Before she followed, Willa poured two glasses of water. One she handed to Samantha, then she held the second up to her *mamm*'s lips.

Mamm managed a couple of sips. *"Denki, dochder."*

Willa sat the water on the floor. "Are you hungry? I have crackers."

Her mother shook her head. "Give the child something, though."

Willa helped Samantha open the cracker packets before she clasped the child's shoulders. "Stay here with my mother and Mr. Erik." The little girl didn't want her to leave, but Willa had to make her understand. "Samantha, this is the safest place for you, and Mr. Mason needs me. He can't fight them off alone." She clasped the child's tiny face and said, "You have been so brave. I need you to stay strong for me and Mr. Mason."

Samantha hugged her. "I will be strong. I promise."

Willa pulled away. "Thank you." She searched

the young girl's face, wishing Samantha didn't have to be so grown-up. "Call out if you need us like you did earlier."

The little girl's frightened eyes held hers for the longest time before she slowly nodded. "I will take care of your mother and Mr. Erik."

This brave child had learned to be strong through all the storms in her life. Willa would, too. "*Denki*, Samantha."

"It will be *oke*." The child parroted the Amish word she'd heard while those stoic brown eyes held so much strength.

Willa smiled. "You said that perfectly." She hugged Samantha close, fighting back tears. If they were unsuccessful, this innocent child would lose her life. There was no room for error, and she had no idea what the outcome would be.

She kissed Samantha's cheek, then let her go. "Thank you for being so brave."

Willa moved to the stairs and looked back in time to see Samantha clutching *Mamm*'s hand. The two of them together filled her with hope.

Upstairs, Willa secured the cellar and covered it with the rug, then went to find Mason. He stood at the side of the window securing a sheet at the top and bottom with nails.

He turned when he heard her come in. "It won't keep them out, but at least they can't see in." He clasped her arm and guided her into the kitchen before extinguishing the lantern. The room around them darkened.

Willa hugged her arms around her body. With the afternoon closing in, the temperature dropped drastically, and she was cold. Not so much from the chill in the air, but from the hopelessness taking root in her heart. Her thoughts went to the ones in the cellar. Would they be warm enough with the quilts she'd brought down? "Let's take a look around back," Mason said. She believed the plan was mostly intended to take her mind off everything.

The view outside the window showed the enclosed buggy and, beyond, the family's old smokehouse slowly crumbling to the ground. It hadn't been used for several years, since before her *daed*'s passing. One of the many things that needed attention.

"Over there." Mason pointed to a man standing on the opposite side of the smokehouse and barely in view. "There's another one at the edge of those trees." He leaned closer. "Wait, that man has a sat phone."

Willa had no idea what he was talking about. "What's a sat phone?"

"A satellite phone. It operates off satellites in the sky instead of towers like regular cell phones. And that's the same man who got away earlier. I'm guessing he's the one in charge." He studied the man for a long moment. "For some reason, the guy who ran away from a fight didn't strike me as Ombra."

Willa got a good look at the man. "He's the one who called the shots when he barged into the house."

Mason let the curtain drop. "Willa, I have an idea, but it's risky." He skimmed her face before telling her. "If I can get to that sat phone, we should be able to make a call."

Her eyes widened. If they could make a call, there was a chance at being saved. "What do you need me to do?" Whatever it was, she would do it.

"I'll need you to cover me. I'm going to try to sneak up on the man with the phone and disable him. Take the phone and his weapon."

"What about the second man? And all the others who might be out of sight?" Surely, they would hear the struggle.

"That's why I need you to cover me. I'll do my best not to make much noise, but if I do, the second man will come to investigate."

Willa understood. She would have to immobilize the second man. "I'll cover you." She didn't hesitate.

He squeezed her arm. "Thank you," he

murmured. "I know it isn't easy." The tenderness she'd seen in him earlier returned to take away the chill from her heart. No matter what the future held, she would always care for Mason. Always remember his courage against so many.

She fought the tears that were close but he saw them.

"Please, don't cry." He put his arms around her. "We're not done yet," he whispered against her ear.

Willa struggled to answer. "I know, but I'm just so angry at these men for what they are doing to Samantha. To us. How can humans be so heartless?"

Mason brushed his hand across her cheek. "I wish I understood the way the world works," he said gently. "I've been gone from the Amish ways for thirteen years, and yet I still don't understand how people can do the things they do to each other. It's discouraging. It makes me…"

He didn't finish, but she wished he had.

Mason leaned his forehead against hers. "I've missed you, Willa. Every time I think of my life here in West Kootenai, you are always there. You make me smile when I remember your tender heart, your gentle strength." His hands fanned her cheeks as he leaned down and kissed her forehead.

Just for a moment, she'd stay close to him and imagine what it might be like to have a future with him.

But only for a moment. "We should hurry," she said in an unsteady voice. "After what just happened, who knows what they'll try next."

His hands fell to his sides. "Are you ready for this?" he said softly, and held her gaze.

She wasn't, but she wouldn't leave him alone. "*Jah*, I'm ready."

"Let me see your weapon." Willa brought out the handgun and handed it to him. He checked the magazine. "You have almost a full clip." He checked his own weapon.

She understood they had a limited window to get the man with the phone incapacitated.

Mason checked the window once more. "He's gone," he said in a surprised tone.

Willa looked over his shoulder. The man with the phone had left the smokehouse. Through the gathering dusk, she searched the woods. "Over there." She pointed. The man had moved to his partner's side. The two were talking.

"I can't afford to let him get away. We need that phone…hold on. There's another man." A third person joined the two. The new man wore an expensive-looking suit and appeared visibly angry. He shoved his finger in both men's faces and raged on. The conversation was barely distinguishable.

"I told you what I expected. Now keep the phone I gave you close in case I need to reach you, and do it." The man with the phone backed away.

Willa's attention returned to the man in the suit. Samantha's words rang through her head. The one who had held her mother wore a suit. This man had been present when Lucian Bartelli killed Samantha's parents. She shivered as she realized the man they were looking at was Ombra.

TEN

"Come on," Mason muttered as he watched the suited man continue to berate the other two. After another lengthy finger-wagging period, the new man turned toward the house. Mason ducked out of sight but not before he'd gotten a good look at the guy in the suit. "I know him," he murmured in stunned disbelief. "What is he doing here?"

"He has to be the one Samantha spoke of. The one who held her mother."

He spun toward her with shock. "That's Dante Bartelli. Lucian's brother. I can't believe it. He helped Lucian kill Samantha's parents. This is huge." As far as the police had been able to determine, Dante was in no way connected to any of his brother's crimes. His only association was being Lucian's high-powered attorney. According to the information they'd uncovered on Dante, the man didn't have so much as a speeding ticket. The truth was beyond terrifying. "Dante Bartelli is Ombra."

"And now that he's here…" She didn't finish, but he read what she didn't say. Now that Dante was here, the real attack would begin.

Dante Bartelli stormed around the corner of the house and out of sight, clearly unhappy with the way his people had handled the situation so far.

Soon, the man with the sat phone returned to his post near the smokehouse. The second moved into the woods and out of sight.

"We have to go now. Before they attack." The stakes had never been higher. He moved to the door. Willa followed.

"It's too risky to go out this way." He glanced around the space, but there was only one option. "I'm going to try and slip out that window. It's on the opposite side from where they are standing guard. I can circle around using the woods until I reach the man with the phone. Take him by surprise." He moved to the window and looked out. "I don't see anyone on this side yet." He wondered how long that would last.

With Willa's help, he removed the nails. Mason slowly raised the window. Before he made a move, Willa grabbed his arm.

"I'm worried it's too dangerous. There could be others in the woods that you can't see."

He understood her concern was for his safety, but without any means of reaching anyone to assist them, it was only a matter of time before they all perished. He couldn't let that happen.

"There's no other way, Willa," he said with a shake of his head. "I have to take the chance."

She slowly nodded. The concern on her face said it all. "I know."

"I'll be careful. Stay by the window at the back near the buggy but out of sight. I may need you to back me up. But keep your eyes open. If they start shooting at the house get down. Don't put yourself in danger of being struck by a bullet."

After he checked a final time to make sure nothing had changed, Mason hoisted himself up and through the opening.

He hit the ground hard and caught himself with his hands. With his pulse pounding in his ears, he glanced around. Not seeing an immediate threat, he rose. Trying to be as quiet as possible, Mason slipped to the back side of the house, flattened himself against the wall and discreetly peered around.

Phone Man stood at the back of the smokehouse, his full attention on the house. From

Mason's vantage point he couldn't see the second man or if indeed there were others around.

There was no way Phone Man wouldn't see him if he tried to reach the buggy from here. He'd have to circle through the woods near this side of the house and back behind the smokehouse if he stood a chance at taking the man by surprise.

He slipped further away from the back and hoped they wouldn't hear him moving into the woods in front of him.

Once he reached the first of the trees, Mason slipped behind one and waited with his heart racing. He half expected Bartelli's men to open fire. When that didn't happen, he moved deeper into the woods and slowly headed through them while trying to be as quiet as possible. He couldn't imagine how frantic Willa must be without having a visual of him yet.

It seemed to take forever before he reached the woods at the back of the smokehouse. Through the leaves, he was able to get a look at the man there. His full attention was on the house. Mason couldn't see the second man. Where was he?

Whether he liked it or not, he had to make his move fast. Mason eased to the edge of the woods. Phone Man still hadn't heard him. This was it. He closed the space between them rapidly. A handful of steps still separated them when the man jerked toward the tiniest sound he made.

The surprise on his face turned to horror in an instant as Mason slugged him with the butt of the weapon. He stumbled backward and hit the side of the smokehouse as he went down.

As hard as Mason tried, the attack hadn't been a quiet one. He acted quickly, searching the man's pocket. Finding the sat phone, he grabbed it and the man's handgun, then started back to the woods.

Before he reached the coverage, the second man rounded the back corner of the building.

The man opened fire. Mason hit the dirt and scrambled for the cover of the smokehouse, then leaned past the corner and returned fire. The man dropped but the damage was done. He'd alerted the rest of Bartelli's people.

Mason took off running through the trees as fast as he could. He had to make it to the house. If they trapped him out in the open, he'd be a dead man.

Out of breath, Mason reached the side of the house and the open window. Through the tree coverage, he could see the smokehouse. Several of Bartelli's soldiers were running that way.

Willa leaned out and grabbed for his hand. "Hurry." With her help, he cleared the opening and collapsed on the floor.

"I was so worried they'd kill you," Willa whispered. She helped him to his feet.

Mason grabbed the hammer and nails and secured the window once more before he hugged her close. "I'm okay. Now we have a way to communicate with the sheriff and not a second too soon."

"The phone." Her expression cleared. "We have a chance."

Relief flowed through his veins when the call went through. He wanted to keep a positive front, but he had a bad feeling. If Bartelli had brought this much manpower to bring down a child, he doubted they'd be afraid to take on the small number of men at the Eagle's Nest sheriff's department.

The dispatcher's voice sounded wonderful. Mason quickly explained their situation. "I need to speak with Sheriff Collins right away." He identified himself and waited only a handful of seconds before the sheriff came on the line.

"Sheriff, this is Marshal Mason Shetler. I have a partner who has been shot and is in bad shape, and I'm trying to protect our six-year-old witness against dozens of men." He told the sheriff where they were. "We need immediate assistance."

The sheriff didn't sound surprised. "I've dispatched four of my deputies your way already. One of your neighbors reported hearing a bunch of gunshots coming from the Lambrights' property. We have an ambulance on its way, as well. Stay out of sight and stay safe, Marshal Shetler. Help is on the way."

Those words had never sounded so good.

"Sheriff, these men are dangerous. They might try to harm your deputies."

"Roger that. I'll make them aware. I'm going to give you my direct cell phone number. If something else breaks, call me right away. Until then, stay safe."

Mason put the number into the phone. "We will. Thank you, Sheriff." He couldn't stop smiling when the call ended. Help was coming. Would it come in time to save them? He saw the same misgiving in Willa, and he did his best to reassure her. "We just have to hold on for a little while longer."

Yet he couldn't get rid of his doubts. There were too many of them to count.

The shooting around back had stopped, and Mason eased himself over to the window. The man whose phone he'd taken had awakened and knelt over his shot partner, screaming at the top of his lungs.

Several men ran to his aid. The man's hands waved wildly as he told them what happened. All eyes focused on the back of the house.

Mason ducked out of sight and returned to the front to search through the shattered window. At least the rain appeared to have stopped for now.

"Let's stay in the kitchen. It's safe." He followed Willa, listening to any sound coming from outdoors. No sirens yet. The drive from Eagle's Nest would take a good half hour. The roads leading into the area were not well maintained. Still, Bartelli's people managed it. The sheriff could, too.

His stomach churned. The sat phone in his hand rang suddenly, causing Willa to jump. Like him, she was on edge.

Looking at the phone, he saw the sheriff's cell phone number and answered it.

"This is Sheriff Collins. We have a problem."

Mason's heart dropped to his stomach. *Bad news*, his head warned while his heart wasn't sure how much more of it they could take and survive.

Willa saw the truth on Mason's face. "How bad is it?" she asked as soon as the call ended.

He ran a hand through his hair. "Bad. The sheriff's men are taking heavy fire." He looked into her eyes. "If they can't make it past Bartelli's people…"

She tried not to break down. "Then it's just us."

"Yes," he said slowly.

Falling apart wouldn't help even though her heart screamed to let go, to stop fighting. Willa shoved down the fears. "Then we'll just have to hold them off until the sheriff and his people can get through."

Mason smiled at her show of courage she didn't really feel. "The house is getting colder by the minute. I'll be right back. I'm going to stir the fire."

He stuffed the phone into his pocket and went to tend to the fire while Willa waited in the kitchen for him. No sound came from the root cellar. Willa prayed Erik's condition hadn't worsened.

Beyond the kitchen curtains, night closed in. The house grew dark. In the distance, shots could be heard. The deputies were fighting a battle themselves.

Mason returned to the kitchen.

"There are so many of them," she whispered.

"Yes. Bartelli's people are trying to hold

the sheriff's men off long enough to finish the job." He looked her way. "Willa…"

She knew what he was going to say, but she didn't want his apologies.

She placed her finger over his lips. "Even if I knew everything that would happen here today, I would still stand by your side and fight for that little girl."

His mouth twisted and he entwined their hands. "You are one strong woman, Willa Lambright. You always were."

He let her hands go and leaned against the counter. "You know, I used to imagine what coming home might look like." A laugh filled with bitterness tore from him. "Believe it or not, this wasn't it."

Her heart went out to him. "I can imagine. This isn't anything I could ever have expected." She sighed and wondered if he'd thought about coming home seriously, or was it just because of what was happening now?

"Do you want to return to West Kootenai?" She squashed the glint of hope before it could take life.

"Many times I've considered it," he said quietly. "To be honest, I've missed so much about this life. I even thought about handing in my badge more than once."

"Do you still think about Miriam?" The

question was out before Willa could stop it. She wished it back as soon as it cleared her lips.

"No, Willa," he said vehemently. "What happened back then was never about me loving Miriam." His expression softened as he skimmed her face. "I was foolish to think it was love, and foolish not to see what was right before me all along." Mason gathered her close and rested his chin against her head. More than anything, she wanted this bittersweet moment to go on forever.

"We'll get through this," he murmured softly. "And when we do…" She held him tighter. He didn't finish and for that she was grateful. Best not to make promises neither could fulfill.

Mason pulled away and looked into her eyes. She couldn't answer a single one of the questions she saw there.

"Willa? What is it? Tell me."

Before the truth could come tumbling from her lips, the world around them exploded.

Mason grabbed her waist and hauled her to the floor beside him, covering her with his body. Beneath them, Samantha screamed. Golden Boy charged up the steps and scratched at the door.

Don't let them win. Don't let us die. Willa prayed with all her heart while the assault raging around them seemed to go on forever.

ELEVEN

He'd expected the attack, braced for it, but nothing prepared him for its magnitude. Mason held Willa close, and he could feel her shaking.

How many men had Bartelli and his brother sent to eliminate the problem? It amazed him that Dante Bartelli wasn't even concerned enough to think twice about engaging the sheriff's deputies. He had to know Sheriff Collins's men would eventually call for backup and force their way through. Was he so sure there would be no one left to save by the time they reached the house?

As hard as he tried, Mason couldn't see a good outcome for anyone in the house. While bullets landed all around, he prayed and wished for another day. Another day with Willa. Another day to make things better for Samantha. Another day to change the things he could with his family.

Just as quickly as it started, the attack came

to an end. For a long moment, he couldn't trust that it was over. He slowly rose from his crouched position and surveyed the room. The window curtain flapped in tattered shreds beyond the busted glass. They'd see him and Willa on the floor. They were in danger every second they were in the kitchen.

"Stay as low as you can and come with me," he said against her ear. Glass lay everywhere on the floor. He clasped her hand and pulled her along beside him until they reached the living room. Was there any room in the house where they'd be safe?

"Where are the sheriff's men?" Willa's voice caught, exposing her terror.

"They're trying. They're doing everything they can."

She swallowed back a sob. "But it may not be in time."

No sooner had the words left her lips than someone tried to kick in the front door.

"We've got to get out of the open." He ushered her behind the sofa realizing it would provide little coverage, but they were running out of options. Once they were out of sight, Mason leaned past the protection of the sofa and fired several rounds into the front door. A loud thud followed. Another man tried to climb through the busted window. All that was visible was his leg, but Mason acted quickly. The bullet struck the exposed appendage, and a scream followed. The man fell backward onto the porch. A second later, stuttered footsteps ran from the house.

Mason stared at the destroyed living room. He didn't have to wait long for the next assault. Several shots came from the back of the house. Bartelli's people were circling the parameter.

He ducked behind the sofa and called the sheriff's cell phone. The call went unanswered.

When quiet settled around them Mason tried the sheriff again without success. How much longer would they be forced to stand alone?

"He's not answering?"

Mason shook his head and placed his arm around her shoulders, holding her close.

Distant fighting reverberated through the countryside. The sheriff and his people were doing everything possible to break through enemy lines.

"I can imagine the sheriff's deputies aren't used to being up against so many."

Mason glanced at the phone still in his hand. For half a second, he thought about reaching out to his supervisor, Owen Harper. Some instinct that didn't make sense warned him not to make that call.

"It's going to work out, Willa. You were

right. God won't let this happen. He won't." But his newfound faith faltered. He'd seen too many bad things through the years. Witnessed Chandler's senseless death. Now a little six-year-old girl was in the fight of her life.

The phone in his hand rang, and Mason quickly answered it, thinking it was the sheriff.

"Is it done?" The voice on the other end was not Sheriff Collins, but he did sound familiar.

Mason tried to think beyond the chaos around him and figure out how he knew this man. "Not yet." He caught Willa's surprise and held a finger to his lips.

"You'd better hurry. They're almost there. Your people can't hold them off forever." The man paused. "This is it. I gave you the information you wanted to find the girl. I'm done. You promised once you had her location, you'd cancel my debt. I took care of your brother's problem. Now you handle mine. We're square."

A moment of silence followed, and then the man appeared to grow suspicious. "Dante? You there? Hello?"

Mason struggled to come up with the right answer. "I'll do what I—"

The phone went dead midsentence. The man had realized he wasn't speaking to the person he thought. The phone at one time had belonged to Dante Bartelli, and the man who called had to be the mole. If they could find the person, it might be possible to tie Dante Bartelli to his brother's crimes.

"Who was that?"

He looked straight at her. "I think I just spoke to the mole."

Willa searched his face. "Are you serious? Did you recognize the voice?"

Did he? Or was he simply grasping for something. "I'm not sure. It sounded familiar, but…" He couldn't be certain. "Why don't you go check on Samantha and Erik and your mother? I'm sure they're all pretty shaken after what happened. I'll keep watch here."

She obviously didn't want to leave him, but he felt uneasy about Erik's condition.

"Go. I'll be fine."

Willa finally let him go and rose. "I'll be right back." Her fingers lingered on his. "Don't you die."

He didn't want to let her go. So many reasons for him to want to live stood before him—in her. "Stay low and out of sight of the window."

She moved to the kitchen, and he heard the trapdoor open. Her soft footsteps faded down the stairs. It felt as if his whole world—his future—went with her.

Mason tried the sheriff again with the same

outcome. With fear closing in, threatening to swallow him up, he hit his knees and prayed with all his heart.

"Help us, Father. I don't know how much longer we can hold out against so many and I'm terrified someone will die. Please place Your protection around us and don't let these bad men take another innocent life."

The "Amen" slipped unsteadily from his lips while a calm he hadn't felt in a long time embraced him. And he realized this was where he was supposed to be. God had placed him here to protect Samantha, and he would do whatever was needed to save her life.

Drawing in air, he rose and kept down as he advanced to the broken window. Nothing appeared in his line of sight. A chill niggled along his backbone.

The trapdoor closed quietly, and Willa returned to the living room. He tried to keep his uneasiness to himself.

"Can you see anything?"

He turned toward her soft voice. "No, nothing so far. How's Erik?"

Her troubled expression confirmed what he already knew, yet she tried to sound positive. "He's sleeping, which is a *gut* thing. He needs rest."

"How're Samantha and your mother holding up?"

"*Mamm* is being herself. Samantha is trying extremely hard to be brave." She smiled and he couldn't take his eyes off her. So beautiful. For so long, he'd pushed aside the life he'd had here in West Kootenai. But lately he found himself remembering the moments spent with his brothers and family, with Willa and hers. And every time he recalled that time, her face made him smile. She'd been the mother hen of the group. The voice of reason. The faithful one.

"She reminds me of you. Kind through and through, but possessing a courage that is stronger than a lot of seasoned law-enforcement agents."

Willa laughed at his description. "Oh, well, there are times when I don't feel so strong." Their eyes connected. "Especially watching my *mamm* go through the things she's endured. Knowing that…" She didn't finish, but he knew what she was thinking.

"I hate this so much," he said. Every time he thought about the monster that was slowly claiming Beth's life, he wanted to rage at someone.

"We'll get through." She misunderstood him.

He claimed her hand. "I don't mean what's

happening now—although I hate it. What I meant is what's happening to Beth isn't fair."

She ducked her head. "No, it isn't. I wish *Gott* would give it to me if it meant she would be free of the disease." He had no doubt she meant every single one of those words.

"And I wish I could make it easier for the both of you."

"I know." She smiled. "*Mamm* loves you so much. She talks about you and your family a lot. Martha visits often, as do your *bruders*. But she talks about you the most because you were always her favorite. *Mamm* never gave up on your returning one day."

It humbled him to think about Beth and so many others praying for him through the years. There were a lot of people who loved him.

He thought about the dream he, Fletcher and Chandler had shared. As *kinner*, they'd been excited to think about owning their own business one day. Something apart from the family one.

Though all his brothers hunted, for him and Fletcher it was more than a way to provide food for the family. The excitement of the hunt. Being outdoors. Using all his skills to complete a successful hunt. For him, the dream hadn't died, even though he'd lost his friend Chandler. He wondered about Fletcher.

Multiple sets of footsteps circling the house broke the quiet around them.

"They're going to try getting inside." As much as he didn't want to put Willa in more danger than he had already, he couldn't fight this battle alone. "Stay behind the sofa. They're coming."

The fear on her face added to his guilt. Mason shoved the bookcase onto the floor and in front of the sofa for added protection. They were buffered on one side by the interior wall to Willa's room. If he peeked around the wall, the back door would be visible. Would it be enough protection to allow them to pick off Bartelli's invading soldiers? His heart pumped adrenaline through his body as he waited for the inevitable.

The front door shook. Mason flipped around and shot. Screams followed.

"Mason." Willa pointed to the window. He turned in time to see her shoot at a man climbing through it. The man quickly retreated.

Outside, what sounded like a four-wheeler in the distance approached between the *Englischer* ranch owned by Ethan Connors and Willa's property. But it was only a single vehicle.

"Did you hear that?" He cocked his head to

one side and listened over the arsenal of shells pounding the house.

"I do. It sounds like Ethan's four-wheeler."

Gunshots were exchanged near the sound. If Willa's neighbor had tried to reach them, he was now under attack.

The assault around the house halted. As bad as he wanted to look outside, Bartelli's men could be waiting.

The fighting behind the house continued to grow closer. Then it stopped. "What happened?" Willa said.

The only noise now came from the shooting where the sheriff's people were near the road, and that appeared sporadic. Relief swept over him. They were gaining ground.

Someone stepped up onto the back porch. A fist pounded against the door. "Mrs. Lambright. Willa. It's Ethan. Can you open up?"

"That's my neighbor." Willa jumped to her feet and ran to the back door.

"Wait, it could be a trick." Mason grabbed her before she shoved the dresser out of the way. He slid to the window and focused on the door. A man dressed in jeans and a sweatshirt, a backpack on his shoulders, waited with his weapon in his hand.

"That's Ethan," Willa confirmed to his relief. "They'll kill him."

Together, they pushed the dresser back enough to open the door. Connors had moved to the corner of the porch and had engaged several shooters to the right of the house. The second he got a break he raced inside the house and slammed the door shut. "Get away from the door. They're coming up fast."

Mason grabbed Willa's arm. Along with Ethan they ducked inside Beth's room seconds before another blitz rattled the house.

"How did you manage to get through?" Mason asked.

"I've been trying to reach you for a while," Ethan told them. "When your mare showed up at my ranch, I recognized her and realized the gunfire came from here. I started out on the four-wheeler, but it caught a bullet. I was forced to come the rest of the way on foot and let me tell you, it wasn't easy avoiding so many armed men. I had to fall back on all my military training to slip past them." Ethan's ashen face reflected the extent of the ordeal he'd faced. "Ethan Connors." He introduced himself to Mason. "I'm Willa's neighbor."

"Boy, are we happy to see you. Mason Shetler. Sorry we have to meet under these circumstances."

Ethan shook his hand. "Same here. You related to Aaron and Eli?"

"I am. They're my brothers."

"I thought so. I see the resemblance. I spoke to the sheriff before attempting this trip." He held up his sat phone. "He's got state troopers on the way, along with law enforcement from all the surrounding counties. Sheriff Collins is bringing four-wheelers into my place in the hopes of reaching you from that direction. They're doing everything to break through, but there are so many shooters out there. Any idea what's happening?"

"Yes." Mason explained the nightmare they'd gone through.

"Bartelli. I recognize the name. That's one bad dude. I heard he's about to stand trial soon."

"Exactly. And our prime witness is six years old and hiding out in Willa's root cellar along with my injured partner and Beth."

And Mason's hope had just about vanished.

Ethan shucked his backpack. "Let me take a look at your partner. I brought some medical supplies with me. From the amount of gunfire taking place around here, I figured someone might be hurt."

"I can take you down," Willa told him, then turned to Mason. "Are you going to be *oke*?"

Mason squeezed her hand. "Yes. Don't worry about me. Take care of Erik."

He watched her go and realized the love growing in his heart for her wasn't new. Willa had always held a special place there. Whenever he thought about his life here, her pretty face beckoned him back. But she had her mother to care for. Her life would always be here in West Kootenai with Beth. Was his?

For years, he'd longed to return to patch things up with his family and find his way back to the community.

But the mess he'd made with his family, the bad decisions that had taken him away from the life he loved—could he ever move beyond them? Ever find forgiveness from his family for them? How could he ask this kind and gentle woman to help him clean up the mess he'd made of his life?

Willa thanked *Gott* for helping Ethan break through Bartelli's soldiers. She and Mason had become battle weary from the endless attacks. Ethan's appearance gave her hope the sheriff and his people would soon follow.

She opened the cellar and descended the steps. The frightened little girl clung to *Mamm*'s hand, her eyes darting past Willa to Ethan.

"You're safe, little one." Willa hurried to the child's side. "This is Ethan. He's a *gut* friend." She kept the child close and waited beside *Mamm*.

"Beth." Ethan acknowledged his friend before he moved to the man lying unconscious on the cot. Dropping to his knees, Ethan opened the backpack.

While he went to work on Erik, Willa leaned down to Samantha's level. "Sweetie, Ethan is going to do everything he can for Erik. Stay here with *Mamm* where it's safe."

Willa let the child go and her mother gathered her close. "How bad is it?" *Mamm* whispered.

She didn't want to mislead her mother, but Samantha could hear everything. Willa didn't want her to know how bad things were. "Pray." She straightened and went over to Ethan. "Can I do anything?"

Ethan's grim expression said it all. He shook his head. "I'll do what I can, but this man needs a hospital right away."

The news confirmed the desperate situation facing them. Life-saving medical attention remained right down the road and unable to break through enemy lines.

She squeezed Ethan's shoulder and returned to the living room where Mason leaned against the bookcase. Weariness clung to his handsome face.

Willa sat beside him. "It's so quiet outside. Do you think the sheriff and his people managed to get through Bartelli's men?"

"I sure hope so," he said in a weary tone. Mason had been fighting these men since early that morning. She wasn't sure how he kept going.

She turned her head and ran her hand across his cheek. "I'm so sorry."

He reached for her hand. "You have no reason to be. I would be dead by now without you. And Samantha would, as well."

Sporadic shooting continued in several directions, yet no sirens.

"What do you think they'll do next? They have to know it's only a matter of time before Sheriff Collins and his people shut them down."

Mason studied their joined hands. "Bartelli won't accept failure, and these men know it." She tried to stay strong. The news was as bad as she thought. "Bartelli's men will fall back from the road. They'll probably leave a few there to attempt to delay the sheriff. The rest will come after us full force. In Dante Bartelli's eyes, these foot soldiers are expendable. He doesn't care how many die or get arrested."

"But if Dante is captured, it could change things. He might turn on his *bruder*." Mason didn't answer and she figured it out. "He's left the area already."

"Probably. If he's gone, there will be no way to connect him to what's happening here."

"But there is. There's us. Samantha. She can now identify him as the one who helped his brother kill her parents..." Willa realized the truth and swallowed back a sob. "He's counting on us not being alive. And none of his men will talk."

Mason slowly nodded. "Exactly. If we're gone and his people are too terrified to talk, there will be no one to connect him with this or any of his brother's crimes."

"Do you think we're going to make it?" If they were going to die, she wanted to hear the truth.

He held her hand against his heart. "I don't know," he managed without looking from her face. "But when it gets bad, I want you to go down to the cellar and wait with the others. Let me handle Bartelli's—"

"Nay." She shook her head and didn't let him finish. "I'm staying here with you. We'll fight them to the bitter end...together."

Mason's beautiful blue eyes held hers a second longer. "Oh, Willa, I so wish I could turn back time." With those words teasing her with possibilities, he leaned in close and touched his lips to hers. His kiss was gentle and yet strong, like the man himself. Her arms circled his neck, drawing him near. No matter what the future held, if they lived and their lives never intersected again, she would remember his kiss for the rest of hers.

He pulled away and leaned his head against her. "I've always cared for you, Willa. I've probably loved you forever."

Words that once would have thrilled her now filled her with sadness. She leaned against his shoulder while she struggled to keep from crying. She'd loved him just as long but lost him to a misunderstanding. She'd always believed that in his heart he felt the same way about her, and yet the truth came too late. And now she couldn't think beyond the pain in her heart.

He put his arm around her and settled her close, his breaths ruffling the escaping tendrils of her hair.

"I'm going to apply for temporary guardianship of Samantha. It will require changing my work schedule, but..." He stopped for a moment. "You asked me once if I was happy with the life I chose. I'm not. But I have the chance to change Samantha's life, and I plan to do everything I can to give her a happy one."

Surprised, she pulled away and searched his face, trying not to show how much the reminder of his leaving affected her. "She will be so happy. Samantha loves you so much. Adopt that little girl. Make her yours. I think you would make a wonderful father." The words caught in her throat and he saw it.

"What's wrong?"

She looked away. This wasn't about her and her foolish wishes. "I'm just happy you are going to be part of Samantha's life."

Too late. Their love came too late.

"A child needs two parents. I can see Samantha really cares for you and your mother."

"Mason…don't," she said, her tone tortured.

"Why? Tell me why?"

How could she put to words the sorrow in her heart?

A sound nearby had them pulling apart. Ethan came into the room. Willa was grateful for his appearance because their discussion would serve no purpose.

"How is he?" Mason asked, his voice rough.

"Holding his own, but the wound is definitely infected." He motioned to the door. "Seems quiet. Any sign of the sheriff?"

"No." Mason shook his head. "And I can't reach him on the phone."

Ethan eased himself to the window and looked out. "I see their police lights. They seem closer."

Mason moved to the window beside Ethan and glanced out while Willa did her best to collect herself.

Why, Gott? *Why bring this to me now?*

She did not wish to think of *Gott* as cruel. He had blessed her life with so many wonderful things. Her *mamm* and *daed.* Her sister, Miriam. Special memories of living in this wonderful community and being friends with the Shetler family, among others. How could she think of *Gott* as cruel? And yet…he'd allowed her *mamm*'s suffering. Without a cure, she most certainly would die before her time. Willa selfishly thought about her life. She would never know the joy of having a *mann* or *kinner* of her own.

"Strange that Bartelli's people aren't taking advantage of the sheriff's absence." Mason frowned. "It doesn't make sense."

"Yeah, to tell you the truth, I don't like it. In battle, quiet usually comes before all-out war."

Ethan's chilling words hung in the air as a man outside yelled, "Attention inside the house!"

Willa hurried to Mason's side.

"Bring the girl out and you'll all live. Don't try to be heroes. You don't get paid enough to die. All we want is the child."

Revulsion rose in Willa's heart. "I can't believe it. They are asking us to trade Samantha for our lives?"

Mason slipped his arm around her shoulders.

"We aren't going to hurt her. We'll take her to a place where she'll have a family to care for her, and she can't cause any more problems. It's what's best for her and you. If you don't bring her out, you all die. The choice is yours."

"It's a lie." Mason's jaw tightened. "They'll kill us all, including Samantha."

A frightening moment passed.

"Last chance," the man called out.

Mason turned Willa to face him. A pulse beat in his jaw. This was the moment they'd been expecting. A second later, the outdoors exploded with gunfire coming from all directions. Mason hit the floor with her. He covered her body with his. "Are you hurt?"

She shook her head and searched for Ethan among the chaos.

The rancher crouched low, protecting his head. "We can't stay here."

"The kitchen," Willa told them.

A moment of peace had them scrambling to their feet. Willa grabbed Mason's hand and started for the kitchen, but stopped when she caught movement out of the corner of her eye.

"Mr. Mason!" Samantha called. The child had heard the noise and fled the cellar.

Mason grabbed the little girl up in his arms. Someone kicked the front door open, forcing them to duck behind the kitchen wall.

The window above the sink shattered with round after round of bullets.

"Keep Samantha with you behind the wall." Mason handed the child to Willa, who gathered the trembling little girl in her arms. Samantha buried her face against Willa and sobbed uncontrollably.

Two men rushed into the house.

Mason and Ethan opened fire. The men dropped.

"Do you hear that?" Ethan turned toward them, a shocked expression on his face.

Over the nightmare taking place around them came a welcoming sound. Sirens.

Mason looked into Willa's eyes. "Help is coming. Stay low to the floor. We just have to hold out a little while longer."

But that wouldn't be an easy task with Bartelli's men pouring into the house.

Mason and Ethan continued to protect them as the multitude of soldiers stormed in.

The entrance to the cellar stood open only a few feet away and yet it might as well be a mile with so much danger all around.

Willa slipped the handgun from her pocket and kept it close while praying with all her heart that *Gott*'s will was for them to be saved.

The battle continued as Samantha clung to Willa and sirens wailed closer.

Several screams came from the living room as Bartelli's men went down, yet more replaced them.

The whole house had become a war zone.

Ethan and Mason crouched low behind the wall and reloaded their weapons.

"I'm almost out," Mason told the man beside him.

"Same here. We have to make each shot count."

Mason scrambled close to Willa, his troubled gaze holding hers. "No matter what, I want you to know I love you."

Her eyes filled with tears. A sob escaped.

Ethan leaned past the wall and opened fire. An onslaught of shots answered. He screamed and fell backward onto the floor. Blood quickly covered the front of his sweatshirt.

"Ethan!" Mason grabbed hold of him and pulled him out of danger.

Willa untangled Samantha's arms.

"No," Samantha moaned when Willa tried to move. "Don't leave me."

"I have to. Ethan needs me." While Mason

continued to hold off Bartelli's men, Willa searched for a safe place for Samantha to hide. She wouldn't be able to safely reach the cellar stairs with all the gunshots spewing through the broken kitchen window. Willa spotted one of the cabinets close enough for the child to reach without being in danger. "See that cabinet there." She pointed to it and the child's tear-filled eyes followed. "Climb inside and don't come out no matter what. My sister and I used to play hide-and-seek in there. You will be safe."

"No, I can't," Samantha sobbed. "It's too far."

"You can. You are strong." Willa opened the cabinet door. "Hurry, Samantha."

The child scrambled from her arms and into the open cabinet. Once she was safely concealed, Willa closed the door and crawled to Ethan. His pained eyes sought hers. She examined his injury.

"It's not so bad." But they both knew differently. Willa slipped off her prayer *kapp* and knotted it up against the wound. "Just rest."

"How is he?" Mason said, tossing his weapon aside and reaching for Ethan's.

"I need something more to stop the bleeding." She looked around the small space where they hid.

"Here, use this." Mason managed to reach a dish towel and handed it to her.

She replaced the bloody prayer *kapp* and applied pressure.

Outside, the sirens screamed closer. Sheriff Collins's people would have another battle on their hands once they reached the house. And until they could clear it, the EMTs wouldn't be allowed inside. Two injured men might die.

Willa struggled to hold back those dark thoughts. It couldn't end like this. Not with lifesaving help a few feet away. Not after they'd battled so hard to live.

Her frightened eyes sought out Mason's. All the same doubts plaguing her were there.

"Don't give up," he whispered, and squeezed her hand. Both glanced at the man lying on the floor. Ethan had tried to save them and now he might die.

Mason dropped her hand as another of Bartelli's men tried to enter the kitchen. He emptied the last of the shells and ducked behind the wall.

"Here, use this one." Willa tossed him her handgun. He quickly checked the clip. "It won't last long." A man entered the kitchen, and Mason whirled and fired.

Willa kept pressure on Ethan's gunshot wound and prayed for the nightmare to end.

The dish towel soon became soaked in blood. Ethan's head slumped sideways. He'd lost consciousness. Mason fought off wave after wave of enemies.

Outside, the sheriff's people engaged Bartelli's soldiers. And more men poured into the house.

TWELVE

The distinct click when he pulled back the hammer confirmed Mason's worst fears. He'd used up all of Willa's bullets and yet the men kept coming. While the battle continued outside, he and Willa wouldn't stand a chance without a weapon.

He eased himself behind the wall's protection. Two men came into the kitchen. Mason dove for one of the dead men's weapons and shot. Both jumped out of the room.

"Stay here," Willa pleaded when he tried to shift the battle away from her and Ethan by going after the men. "Let the sheriff handle them."

He looked into her eyes and read all the things she wanted to say. "We don't have that long. Take care of Samantha and Ethan."

Tears shone in her eyes. Before she could say anything, Mason started for the opening, keeping low. Someone fired. He tucked against the wall and waited for the shooting to stop.

The chaos taking place in the house made it hard to see clearly.

"Mason, watch out," Willa yelled.

A man appeared only a few inches away and shoved the weapon in his hand against Mason's side. Before Mason had time to react, Bartelli's soldier pulled the trigger. A bullet ripped through Mason's body. He stumbled forward, holding on to his weapon with difficulty.

"No," Willa screamed. She reached him and grabbed his gun, then fired at the enemy. Mason staggered on his feet. The world around him blurred. He was losing consciousness. He slammed into the door frame. Slid to the floor while the shot throbbed through his injured body.

He became aware of gunshots flying all around. Willa tried to drag him out of the line of fire while her frightened eyes held his.

"I've got you, Mason, I've got you. You will be *oke*." But the pain coursing through his body indicated otherwise.

Bullets sprayed through the kitchen. Willa hauled him deeper into the room and waited out the onslaught before she continued to pull him deeper into the kitchen and out of danger of the gunfire.

While he tried to get enough air into his lungs, all he could think about was Willa and his youngest witness.

The shooting outside seemed less frequent. The sheriff was gaining control.

Mason's gaze landed on the cabinet where Samantha had hidden. The door stood open. "Where's Samantha?" He managed to get the words out. Willa jerked toward it.

"Samantha!" she screamed, and frantically searched the kitchen. "They have her."

Mason grabbed his side and stumbled to his feet, trying to stay focused. Samantha needed him.

Putting one foot in front of the other took all his concentration. Willa moved to the kitchen entrance. "I don't see anyone." She turned back to him. "Wait here for me. I'll find Samantha." She slipped from the room while all sorts of bad outcomes ran through his head.

"I'm coming with you," he murmured to himself as he lost his footing and fell hard. Grabbing his side, he tried to breathe through the pain. The injury slowed him down, but the battle wasn't over. Samantha. He wasn't about to let Bartelli and his people hurt her. He had to get up. Keep fighting. Through the haze of blood loss, he heard more sirens headed their way. The ambulances had been dispatched. It was almost over.

Gripping his side, he forced himself up to his knees and then to his feet. Crossing the room seemed to take all his energy. Another of Bartelli's soldiers lay dead near the kitchen entrance. Mason inhaled painfully, leaned down and grabbed his weapon.

He stumbled from the room. He had to keep it together for a little while longer. Had to find the little girl who he'd promised to protect.

None of Bartelli's men were in the living room. The house had been teeming with them earlier. They must have realized the sheriff's men had gotten control.

Where was Samantha? Willa's midsection tightened. She raced to the open front door. Her frantic gaze searched the porch. Nothing but a wave of police officers. Bartelli's soldiers wouldn't take the child out that way. Which left the back door.

She ran toward it. Through the darkness in the house, a man dragged Samantha along with him.

The child's frantic gaze latched on to Willa's. "H-help me," Samantha whimpered.

Willa pointed the handgun at the man. "That's far enough. Let her go."

He stopped dead and whirled toward her. A gun was placed near Samantha's head. "She's coming with me." A nasty grin spread across his face. "And you can't stop me." He moved closer to the door.

"Stop or I will shoot," Willa warned. No matter what, she wouldn't let this man leave with Samantha.

He kept the weapon trained on Samantha.

She was now in a standoff with an armed man who wouldn't think anything of killing Samantha and her.

Though terrified, Willa stood her ground, kept the weapon pointed at the man's head and edged toward him. "Let. Her. Go." Samantha's frightened gaze never left Willa's. "It's *oke*, sweetie. I'm not going to let him hurt you." And she wasn't. Even if she had to take a bullet. She'd protect Samantha to the death.

Willa breathed deeply. A surprised expression showed on the man's face as he glanced past her to something else. She never took her focus off him as she aimed. But the shot didn't come from her. The man's eyes snapped shut and the weapon fell from his hand to the floor. His hold on Samantha released, and the little girl ran straight for Willa. She gathered the child behind her as the man tumbled to the floor with a loud thud.

"Oh, thank You, *Gott*." The prayer flew from Willa's lips. With Samantha clinging to her side, she grabbed the man's weapon and tucked it into her apron, then she spun toward where the shot had come from. Mason. He lay on the floor near the kitchen opening, and he wasn't moving. Willa ran toward the man who meant so much to her.

She dropped to the floor beside him as his glazed eyes stared into hers.

"Mr. Mason, please don't die." Samantha wrapped her tiny arms around his waist and sobbed against his chest.

Willa gently extracted the child's arms. "He's not going to die. I won't let him." She wasn't sure if she'd said it for Samantha or herself. Willa set the gun beside her and quickly removed her apron. She wadded it up against the wound.

Please send help now.

Several people stepped into the house. Holding back tears, Willa grabbed the weapon before she realized it was the sheriff and two of his deputies.

"Over here!" she called out.

The three spotted her. "Get the EMTs in here now," the sheriff told the female deputy at his side.

Sheriff Collins and his second deputy closed the space between them.

"Ma'am, my deputy is a former EMT," the sheriff told Willa. "Let him help."

The deputy took over while Willa and Samantha huddled close to Mason.

"There is an injured man in the kitchen and another in the cellar." Willa did her best to stay calm and explain the men's injuries.

Two EMTs hurried into the house and worked on getting Mason stabilized while others went to assist Ethan and Erik.

The sheriff took Willa and Samantha aside. "Where's your mother?"

She struggled to pay attention to what he asked. All she could think about was Mason. "She's in the cellar with Erik. She's suffering from Huntington's disease. This has been hard on her."

The sheriff nodded. "We'll have someone take a look at her, as well."

Willa couldn't stop shaking.

"What about you and the little girl. Are you hurt?" The sheriff leaned down to Samantha's level. "Honey, why don't I have someone take a look at you?"

Samantha shrank against Willa's skirt. Willa held her tight.

"She's just frightened. Otherwise unhurt."

The sheriff straightened. "And you?"

Her? She wasn't sure. Willa glanced around at the devastation that had once been her home and all she could think about was Mason. After everything they'd gone through, she still loved him. With all her heart she loved him. And he loved her. Yet his injury was severe, and the things that stood between them seemed insurmountable.

The EMTs working on Mason lifted the gurney. They were ready to transport him to the hospital.

Both Ethan and Erik were brought out to additional waiting ambulances.

"I'm going with Mason, but I want to check on my *mamm* first." With Samantha clinging to her hand, Willa hurried down the steps of the cellar to where her mother was sitting up in her chair.

Mamm spotted Willa and her face lit up. "I've been so worried about you, *dochder*. There were so many shots."

Willa hugged her mother. "Mason's hurt." She fought against tears.

Mamm clutched her hands. "Go with him. I'll be fine here."

Willa shook her head. "How can I leave you?"

The female deputy who had been waiting

with *Mamm* came over. "I told your mother we'd like to take her to the hospital to check her out just to make sure everything is well. With her health condition and after what's happened, I'd feel better if you'd let us take you in," she said to *Mamm*.

"She's right. You've been through a lot." Willa faced the deputy. "Can we take her with Mason?"

The deputy glanced up the steps. "Let me check. I'll be right back."

Willa glanced down at herself covered in Mason's blood. "I can't believe what has happened." She held Samantha close and prayed the girl would not have to go through anything like this again.

The deputy returned. "We have room for you, ma'am."

The EMTs brought a stretcher down for her mother then gently lifted her onto it and carried her up the steps. Willa and Samantha followed them out to the ambulance.

"Thank you." Willa turned back to the deputy. "I am sorry. I don't know your name."

"Megan Clark, and you're welcome." The woman smiled. "Our deputies and crime scene techs will be here for a while as we process the scene."

The damage to the house would take months

to repair. The emotional scars much longer for this child at her side.

"You're safe now," the deputy assured her. "Most of Bartelli's men are in custody."

But until Bartelli was in prison for good, along with his *bruder*, Samantha remained in danger.

Willa helped the child into the ambulance, then followed. Behind them, the sheriff had a police escort traveling with them to keep Samantha safe.

Willa watched the EMT monitor Mason's vitals. He had lost consciousness, and he appeared so pale from loss of blood.

She fought to keep from falling apart. A hand covered hers. She turned to see her *mamm* watching her.

"Pray, child. *Gott* will listen."

Willa nodded and wiped the tears away. She closed her eyes and poured out her heart to *Gott*.

Please don't take him. Not after everything he did to protect this precious kinna.

She prayed for Erik and Ethan as the ambulance's sad siren screamed through the dark night.

As soon as they reached the hospital, Mason was taken away to surgery. Willa and Samantha, along with their police escort, went with *Mamm* to be examined.

"Is Mr. Mason going to be okay?" the little girl asked while she and Willa waited for news on *Mamm*.

Willa looked into those guiltless eyes and did her best to reassure the young child that another adult she loved wouldn't die.

"He's a strong man and the doctors are going to do everything they can."

Mamm's doctor stepped from the room to speak with Willa. "I'd like to keep her overnight just to be on the safe side, especially after everything that happened at your home. I'm giving her an IV drip to help boost her strength. Your mother has been telling me what you all went through. It sounds absolutely horrifying." The doctor's gaze slipped over Willa's soiled clothing. "And from the looks of you, I can't even imagine."

They'd gone through things that nightmares were made of and she hoped none of them would ever have to go through that again.

"You can head in and see her now if you'd like."

Willa smiled gratefully. "I would."

"I'll stop back later to check on her."

"*Denki*, Doctor." With Samantha's hand

in hers, she stepped into the room where her mother lay on the bed, an IV hooked to her arm.

"How are you feeling?" Willa asked once they reached her bedside.

"Gut." She indicated the IV. "Whatever is in this has helped." She smiled down at Samantha. "Is there news on Mason and the others?"

"Not yet." And Willa couldn't stop worrying.

"You should go check on them. I will be fine."

Willa hesitated. "Are you sure?"

"I am. Go. I think I'll shut my eyes for a second. It's been a long day."

Willa squeezed her mother's arm. "That it has."

"I want to come with you," Samantha pleaded.

With her *mamm* resting peacefully, Willa took Samantha with her, police officers trailing behind for their protection, and went to check on Mason.

"He's still in surgery, miss. As are Mr. Connors and Marshal Timmons. If you want to have a seat in the waiting area, I'll have the doctor come speak with you as soon as there's news."

"Denki." Though not the news she hoped for, as the saying went, no news was *gut* news.

Willa found a chair near the nurses' station. Samantha climbed up in her lap and wrapped her tiny arms around Willa's neck. Tears filled Willa's eyes at the child's soft breath. Though she had only known Samantha for a short time, she loved her and worried about her future. She prayed Mason would be able to act as Samantha's guardian.

"I wish I didn't have to leave you and Mr. Mason. I like it at your house. I wish we could all stay with you there forever."

The tiny confession was torture to hear. This little girl had worked her way into Willa's heart. She'd give anything to be able to keep Samantha with her and have her grow up in the simple Amish world and hopefully away from any future violence.

Samantha snuggled close as the hours slipped by and Willa continued to pray with all her heart for Mason and the other wounded men.

"Are you here for Marshal Shetler?" a male voice spoke quietly nearby. Willa jerked toward the sound. A man in a white coat stood next to her.

"I am." She slowly rose with Samantha in her arms.

"I'm his doctor. He's back in his room now

and he's awake. The surgery went well. You can see him if you'd like."

Thank You, Gott. Her heart rejoiced.

She sat Samantha on her feet and clasped her hand. "*Jah,* I would." Willa noticed several people heading their way. Two wore deputy uniforms. The man and woman with them were dressed in *Englischer* clothing. Willa recognized the two deputies. She didn't know the others.

"Samantha, hi, I'm Marshal Warren." The woman introduced herself and then turned to the man beside her. "And this is Marshal Harris." She looked down at Samantha. "We're going to be protecting you for a while until Marshal Shetler is able to take over again."

Willa remembered Mason telling her there was a mole within the marshal service. "I'm sorry, but I'm not letting you anywhere near this child."

Samantha buried herself against Willa's side.

Marshal Warren's attention went to Willa. "I realize you don't trust us, but I can assure you, we are here to protect Samantha and you."

Still, after everything they'd been through, Willa couldn't let her guard down for a moment.

She spotted Sheriff Collins coming toward

them and told him her fears. At this point he was one of the few people she trusted.

"They've been cleared," he assured her. "I spoke to Marshal Shetler's commander, who is here at the hospital by the way. They have the mole in custody. You can trust these two marshals."

Relief swept the last of her doubts away. "*Denki*, Sheriff." She wasn't sure how much more drama she could take. Willa faced the two marshals again. "I'm Willa Lambright. Marshal Shetler and his partner were at my house when Bartelli's men tried to hurt Samantha."

Marshal Warren nodded. "We have our people helping the sheriff out with the investigation."

"I have several of my people watching the entrances and guarding Marshal Shetler and Marshal Timmons, along with Ethan Connors," the sheriff told her.

The added protection was reassuring. "We're on our way to see Marshal Shetler now." Willa glanced down at Samantha. "Can I take Samantha to see him? She's been worried."

"Of course," Marshal Harris answered. "We'll be right outside the door if you need anything."

They went with the doctor to Mason's room.

"What about the two men who were brought in at the same time?" Willa asked him.

The doctor's smile brought immediate relief. "Both are recovering from their injuries. They should be fine. Someone definitely watched out for you all tonight."

Willa couldn't agree more.

THIRTEEN

Mason couldn't believe what his commander told him. "Your son?" Still groggy from surgery, he hoped he'd heard Owen wrong. "Why would Patrick do such a thing?" He had to know why so many lives had been put in jeopardy. Why Samantha had almost died, and his partner and Ethan had suffered.

Owen Harper appeared to be a defeated man. He'd arrived at the hospital while Mason was still in surgery. As soon as the doctor gave him permission, Owen told Mason everything. The mole Mason and Erik had suspected was none other than Owen's son, Patrick.

"He got mixed up in gambling," Owen said with a shake of his head. The tragedy of what happened had to be horrific for a father to learn. "I think Bartelli may have deliberately targeted him because he knew Patrick was my son, and he figured he could use him to get information on Samantha's safe houses...and he did." Owen exhaled wearily. "Patrick came to me a couple of hours ago and told me everything. I had to arrest my own son." His voice broke.

Mason's heart went out to his friend. "That must have been hard." But another piece of the puzzle fell into place. The man who called the sat phone. Mason realized why he thought he recognized him. He'd met Patrick many times.

"Patrick will cooperate. With his testimony and Samantha's, we can put Lucian Bartelli away for a long time."

Good news, but another Bartelli deserved to go to prison. Mason told him about Dante's part in what happened. "Dante is Ombra. And I believe he's the one who forced Patrick to cooperate for the very reasons you suspect." He explained about the odd call he'd received on the sat phone. "Dante mentioned giving the phone to the man we took it from."

"So, Patrick thought he was calling Dante. Unbelievable. I'll get started on an arrest warrant for Dante. Let's see if he'll remain loyal to his brother or sell him out." Owen held his gaze. "I've assigned two marshals to watch over Samantha until this is over. We'll need to get her to a safe house. You have any place in mind?"

He did. "Somewhere here in West Kootenai.

She'll be frightened and she's been through enough. I want to be part of everything connected to her protection. I love that little girl."

Owen's surprise was obvious. Getting too close to a witness could be dangerous for everyone involved. But this was different. Mason wasn't going to let Samantha be put into the foster system and he told Owen what he wanted. Owen's wife worked for Child Protective Services. Mason hoped she could help.

"I'll speak with Denise and Samantha's caseworker and see what we can do. You might have to make some changes to your work, like taking a desk job. The child will need a lot of attention."

Mason hesitated. He'd been searching for something for a long time. He just hadn't realized that what he'd been looking for was what he'd left behind. More than anything, he wanted to make changes to his life. Just not the ones Owen spoke of.

Mason gathered his strength and told his friend everything.

For the longest time, Owen didn't speak. "Are you sure this is what you want? You've been through something life-changing. Maybe you should give it time."

Mason shook his head. "It wouldn't change my mind. I know what I want, and it's the life

I left behind." And the woman whose memory had always brought a smile to his face.

Someone knocked on his door. Willa stepped into the room along with Samantha.

The child's eyes lit up when she spotted him. Samantha ran to his bedside. "Mr. Mason, you're awake."

Though he still had a long road of recovery ahead, the sight of Samantha put a smile on his face. He grabbed her tiny hand in his. "I am, and I'm going to be just fine."

Mason looked to the woman who hovered near the door, her dark blue dress stained with his blood. Her hair was uncovered and falling from her bun. She watched him with uncertain eyes. They'd haunted him so much through their years apart. And she'd never been more beautiful.

He held out his hand to her.

Willa slowly crossed the room to his side and clutched his hand. "I was so worried."

He didn't look away. "I know."

Owen cleared his throat and Mason introduced them to his commander.

Owen shook Willa's hand and smiled at the child. "Looks like you are already on your way to gaining her affection." He pointed to Samantha before starting for the door. "I'm going to check on Erik. I'll stop by later to see you.

It was nice to meet you, Willa." With a nod for Mason, Owen left them alone.

Mason struggled to find the right words.

"I spoke to the doctor who treated you. Erik and Ethan are both going to be *oke*," she said when the silence lengthened between them.

Samantha climbed up in bed beside him. Despite the pain of her movements, he was happy to have her close. He loved her...and he loved Willa. But would she forgive him for making the wrong choice all those years earlier? Did she love him back? He believed she did.

"I'm leaving the marshals service, Willa." The words came out in a rush. He hadn't meant to say it like that.

"You are? But why?" Her brows gathered together as she stared at him.

"Because I haven't been happy for a long time. Truth be told, I've never really found fulfillment in my work since I left West Kootenai." He tried to understand what she might be thinking, but that frown gave nothing away.

"I made a mistake by leaving. By letting the guilt I felt over Chandler's death fester for so long. If I'd dealt with what happened instead of pushing it aside, I wouldn't have overreacted to what happened between Eli and Miriam. I would have seen it as the blessing it was meant to be." He stopped for air. "And that my heart belonged to someone else."

Her eyes widened. Tears hovered there, yet she remained silent. What if he'd misjudged things? What if all she wanted from him was friendship?

"What I'm doing a really bad job of saying is I should have seen the truth back then. It was always you and me—not Miriam."

He tugged her closer.

"Mason…"

"I'm saying I love you, Willa. I guess I always have. There were too many other things getting in the way of me seeing the truth until now."

"Mason…"

"But I do love you. So much."

Tears spilled from her eyes and she tried to pull away, but he wouldn't let her. "What is it?"

She didn't speak.

"Willa, I think you have feelings for me. I know I've made a mess of things, and I have a long way to go to be able to return to the Amish faith completely, but I want to, and I will because I want to marry you." And he wanted to make Samantha part of their family.

A sob escaped and she turned away. "I can't marry you, Mason."

His world collapsed. "Tell me why. Is it me?"

Her mouth twisted in pain. "No, it's not you. How could it be you?"

"Then what? Let me fix it."

"Oh, Mason." She wiped tears from her cheeks and sat beside him. "You can't fix this. No one but *Gott* can fix it."

He stared at her for the longest time before he figured it out. "It's your mother's disease. It can be inherited."

Willa nodded. "There's a test to see if I have it, but I'm scared. I haven't taken it yet because I'm not sure I want to know."

He cupped her cheek. "Whether or not you have Huntington's doesn't matter to me."

"But it does to me. How can I ask you to watch me go through what *Mamm* is struggling with? How can I saddle you with such a burden?"

He loved her so much he would do anything in the world for her. Even take her illness if it were possible.

"Willa, if working as a marshal has taught me anything, it's that none of us are guaranteed another day." He glanced down at Samantha, who had glued herself into the crook of his arm, content to listen to the grown-ups talk about things she didn't understand.

"We have now. This time. And I want to spend it—however long it is—with you. It doesn't matter what the future holds. If we're together, we'll get through whatever life throws our way." He paused to look into her eyes. "Please let me share your future."

A sob escaped, and she stared at him for a long moment before she leaned down and kissed him gently.

Samantha covered her face at the expression of love, and Mason chuckled.

"I love you, Mason. I've loved you since... well, forever." Willa was crying but also smiling. "And the thought of putting you through what I've watched *Mamm* suffer with is horrible."

"It doesn't matter. None of it matters as long as we are together." He inhaled and was glad he'd been right about her feelings for him. "I love you, Willa Lambright. Will you share your future with me? Will you marry me?"

A radiant smile spread across her face and her eyes sparkled with happiness. "Yes, oh, yes."

His heart soared. The future never seemed brighter.

"You've made me so happy," he said. "And if everything works out well, then we will have a *kinna* to share our lives with us." He mouthed the last because he didn't want to get Samantha's hopes up yet. When he had the go-ahead from the child's social worker, he'd tell her.

Until the trial and Lucian Bartelli's imprisonment, Samantha would require protection. Though he and Erik would not be physically able to safeguard the child, he planned to be part of every decision regarding her safety.

He prayed Samantha would be allowed to share their happiness, because if anyone needed the love he and Willa could give her, it was this beautiful child.

A tap on the door had them both turning.

It opened and the past he'd left behind came pouring in.

His mother hurried to his side. "Mason, oh, my boy." Her words came out in a sob as she bent down and hugged him close while Samantha watched with big eyes. "We received news from Sheriff Collins you were hurt." His mother wept openly.

"I'm fine, *Mamm*. Don't worry."

Willa smiled and stepped aside to let his family draw close. Soon, she and her *mamm* would be part of Mason's wonderful family. And maybe, just maybe, Samantha, as well.

Mason clutched his mother's hand. It had been several years since he'd seen this precious woman, and he couldn't take his eyes off her.

She turned to the family gathered around.

His brothers. Each face held love for him that he would do everything he could to be worthy of receiving.

The eldest, Aaron, stepped forward. "It's *gut* to see you again, *bruder*. I wish it was under different circumstances, but we're happy you're home." A pretty blonde woman held a toddler in her arms. At her side stood a young man who had to be Caleb, Aaron's son.

"This is my *fraa*, Victoria, and our *dochder*, Katie. And you may not recognize my *sohn*. He has shot up into a fine young man."

Mason greeted Victoria and couldn't get over how much Caleb had grown since last he'd seen him.

At the back of the group, past his brothers Hunter and Fletcher, stood the one he'd hurt the most. Eli. His brother who he had treated so badly had come to see him.

"Eli. Thank you for coming."

Eli came to his side. With him was a woman who appeared familiar and noticeably pregnant. "I'm glad to see you, *bruder*." Eli hugged him before he turned to the woman at his side. "This is Faith. She and I have been married for almost a year now."

Mason was speechless. "I'm pleased to meet you, Faith. You look so familiar."

Faith chuckled and shook his hand. "That's

because I grew up here in West Kootenai until I turned ten. I remember you well. You were always urging your *bruders* to be adventurous."

Mason cringed. "That's why we were always in trouble."

This was the first time he and Eli had spoken since that time long ago, but he didn't want it to be the last. "I'm sorry, *bruder*. I drove you and Miriam away when I shouldn't have." Mason swallowed several times. Regrets weighed heavy on his shoulders, but he couldn't rewrite the past. All he could do was make it up to his brother.

Eli clasped his arm. "We all made mistakes. The past is finished, but the future is wide-open."

Mason looked to Willa. "Yes, it is." And he was so ready to jump into it with her at his side, and with this precious child who obviously wasn't sure what to make of the crowd of people around her. But she would. In time. They would become her family, too, and he looked forward to both him and Samantha getting to know his grown-up brothers...with Willa at his side.

EPILOGUE

Eighteen months later...

Willa stopped at the door to her *mamm*'s room and listened. The giggling had been going on for quite a while.

She stuck her head into the room. "All right, you two?"

Samantha glanced up from the book she had been reading to her *grossmammi*.

The love Samantha and Willa's *mamm* shared always warmed her heart. Though her mother had her bad days, Willa believed it was thanks to Samantha's gentle love more than the medication prescribed that *Mamm*'s condition had not worsened in the past months.

Today was a special day, and Willa had baked two pies, cleaned the kitchen until it shone and scrubbed all the floors before lunch because she couldn't stop worrying. Today, she and Mason would find out if they became the official *mamm* and *daed* for young Samantha.

In the year and a half since the nightmare of the attack on her home had happened, Willa's life had changed so much.

For a time, she and *Mamm* had gone to live with Mason's mother while his *bruders* repaired her family home.

Mason had been able to pull some strings and become Samantha's guardian. Then, when she and Mason married, Samantha came to live with them and *Mamm*.

He and his *bruder* Fletcher had fulfilled their lifelong dream with the help of Ethan Connors. Their hunting guide business continued to gain new clients each season. They'd even helped rescue several lost hikers last fall when an unexpected snowstorm caught them unprepared.

And Samantha had been so brave. She'd gone to court and pointed out the man who killed her parents. Thanks to her testimony, along with Owen's son's, Lucian Bartelli would spend the rest of his life in prison. Dante hadn't remained loyal to his brother. He'd sold Lucian out. No honor among thieves.

Bartelli's empire had crumpled. Samantha was safe at last.

The nightmare the child had gone through

was slowly fading with time. Samantha kept a picture of her family in her room. Willa wanted her to remember them.

But today things might be changing. Would Samantha be theirs for real? Willa had prayed so hard. On her knees, pouring out her heart while scrubbing floors. And then she'd prayed some more.

She placed a tray of food on the bedside table. "You want to take your lunch with *Grossmammi*?" she asked, though she knew the answer.

"Jah." Samantha said the word and giggled. She was slowly learning their language. Willa was so proud of her.

"That's perfect." The child beamed at her praise.

She handed a plate of meat loaf, green beans and mashed potatoes to the little girl.

"Shall we pray?" Willa waited until Samantha had bowed her head before she told all her fears to *Gott*.

Please don't take her from us. We love this little girl so much. And she loves us.

"Amen," Willa whispered in an unsteady tone that only *Mamm* understood.

"Why do they call it a silent prayer? Why don't we pray out loud?"

Willa looked to her mother, who smiled adoringly at the child.

"Because we believe our prayers are for *Gott* to hear alone. They are between Him and us."

Samantha accepted her *grossmammi*'s answer and dug into her favorite meal.

Though Willa had taken the test and learned she would be spared her mother's diagnosis, not a day went by when she didn't wish she could take it from her *mamm*.

While she did not understand *Gott*'s way in this, she would treasure each day she had with this wonderful woman who had taught her so much, and she would love her for as long as *Gott* allowed them to be together.

Mamm mouthed, "Any news?"

Willa shook her head. She helped her mother with the meal and talked about what she'd been doing.

"Samantha, did you tell *Grossmammi* how you mastered the craft of milking?" Willa glanced at the child.

"I milked Buttercup all by myself," she said proudly. "*Mamm* said I could do it every time as long as I made sure she was there. She said Buttercup sometimes takes a while to get used to new people, but we're friends already."

Willa suppressed a smile. "She's becoming very helpful around the place." Her voice broke off as she thought about the possibility of losing the young girl. She loved Samantha so much. She couldn't imagine her life without this beautiful child in it. "I'm going to teach you how to cook next."

Mamm had tears in her eyes. "I can't wait to taste her wonderful dishes."

Samantha took a bite of food and frowned when she saw the tears. "Why are you crying?"

Mamm shook her head. "No reason. I'm just so happy."

Willa turned away to brush off her own tears.

A noise outside grabbed her attention. A buggy was coming their way. Mason had returned.

"I'll be right back." Willa caught her mother's troubled expression before she left the room and hurried through the house to stand on the porch.

Mason urged the buggy down the path toward her. She couldn't tell anything from his expression. He pulled the buggy in front of the barn and she hurried down the steps to his side.

By the time she reached her *mann*, he was on the ground. She stopped a few feet away and searched his eyes.

A smile spread across his face and she ran into his arms.

"She's really ours?" Willa whispered in between sobs.

"She's ours." He held her close while all the tension left her body.

"I was so worried." Willa looked at him and smiled before she kissed him tenderly.

"I know. Me, too. My hands were shaking the entire time. But she's ours and no one is going to hurt her again."

The strength in those words had been there many times before. Every time he spoke about Samantha, that fierce protectiveness filled his tone.

Willa couldn't stop smiling. If she had been told it was possible to be this happy the year before Mason returned, after her *daed*'s death and her mother's deteriorating disease, she couldn't have imagined it.

Gott had shined his blessings on them. She had not only gained a husband but a brand-new family, as well—filled with *bruders* and sisters, and a mother-in-law who proved so caring. Her life was full.

"I love you, Mason. I'm so happy." She went into his arms and held him close. Samantha was their child.

He smiled and kissed the tip of her nose. "Let's go tell Samantha and your *mamm*. I can't wait to see their faces."

There might be clouds on the horizon, but today would be a day filled with joy.

Together, they stepped into *Mamm*'s room, and her worried eyes found Willa's. She hurried to her mother's side and hugged her tight. "She's ours," she whispered. "No one is going to take her from us."

Her mother's frail body quaked with sobs. While Willa held her tight and tried not to cry, as well, Samantha noticed her *grossmammi*'s tears and hurried to her side.

"What's wrong, *Grossmammi*? Are you sad?"

Willa turned to her daughter and answered, "She's not sad, *kinna*, she's happy." Willa looked to Mason, who scooped Samantha up into his arms.

"What your *mamm* means is you are our daughter. I went to court today and asked the judge to let you stay with us forever. He said yes."

Willa waited and hoped Samantha would be as happy with the news as they all were.

"Like when I had to go and sit in the chair and tell them what happened?" The child rarely talked about having to testify or the time when her parents had died. For a long time, there were nightmares. Willa spent many a night holding her daughter while she cried. But lately, those times were few.

"Yes, like that." Mason kept his answers simple so Samantha could understand.

"And they said I could stay here. I don't have to leave?" The little girl with the solemn eyes held Mason in her spell.

"Yes, that's right. You are our daughter. No one will take you away from us." He waited for a reaction.

Her tiny face broke into a smile and Samantha hugged his neck. "I'm so happy, *Daed*."

Willa's eyes widened at Samantha's use of the word for *father*. She'd been practicing the word for some time. She'd called Willa *Mamm* for a while now but had struggled with the word for *dad*. What a perfect day to say it properly.

Mason's eyes flew to hers. "She called me *Daed*."

Laughter bubbled from deep inside Willa. "She did, and she said it perfectly."

Not long ago, Willa's future had been plagued with darkness and doubts. Now she had more than her heart's desire, and she was looking forward to each new day that came her way. With the boy who had become the man she loved with all her heart.

* * * * *

If you enjoyed this story,
don't miss Mary Alford's next
Amish romantic suspense,
available next year from
Love Inspired Suspense!

Find more great reads at
www.LoveInspired.com.

Dear Reader,

I find myself reminiscing about childhood things a lot lately. Reliving some of the happy and, yes, silly moments from that time brings a smile to my face. It was a simpler time. A different world.

For Mason Shetler, it takes coming back to his childhood Amish community to realize how special that life once was for him. Through the courage found in a little girl who has lost everything, and the strength of a woman whose future is uncertain, Mason discovered what he had been searching for all along.

I truly hope you enjoy Mason and Willa's fight to protect young Samantha and the love they find along the way. And I hope their happy ending leaves you with a smile.

Blessings always,
Mary Alford

Get 4 FREE REWARDS!

We'll send you 2 FREE Books plus 2 FREE Mystery Gifts.

Harlequin Heartwarming Larger-Print books will connect you to uplifting stories where the bonds of friendship, family and community unite.

FREE Value Over $20

YES! Please send me 2 FREE Harlequin Heartwarming Larger-Print novels and my 2 FREE mystery gifts (gifts worth about $10 retail). After receiving them, if I don't wish to receive any more books, I can return the shipping statement marked "cancel." If I don't cancel, I will receive 4 brand-new larger-print novels every month and be billed just $5.74 per book in the U.S. or $6.24 per book in Canada. That's a savings of at least 21% off the cover price. It's quite a bargain! Shipping and handling is just 50¢ per book in the U.S. and $1.25 per book in Canada.* I understand that accepting the 2 free books and gifts places me under no obligation to buy anything. I can always return a shipment and cancel at any time. The free books and gifts are mine to keep no matter what I decide.

161/361 HDN GNPZ

Name (please print)

Address   Apt. #

City   State/Province   Zip/Postal Code

Email: Please check this box ☐ if you would like to receive newsletters and promotional emails from Harlequin Enterprises ULC and its affiliates. You can unsubscribe anytime.

Mail to the Harlequin Reader Service:
IN U.S.A.: P.O. Box 1341, Buffalo, NY 14240-8531
IN CANADA: P.O. Box 603, Fort Erie, Ontario L2A 5X3

Want to try 2 free books from another series! Call 1-800-873-8635 or visit www.ReaderService.com.

*Terms and prices subject to change without notice. Prices do not include sales taxes, which will be charged (if applicable) based on your state or country of residence. Canadian residents will be charged applicable taxes. Offer not valid in Quebec. This offer is limited to one order per household. Books received may not be as shown. Not valid for current subscribers to Harlequin Heartwarming Larger-Print books. All orders subject to approval. Credit or debit balances in a customer's account(s) may be offset by any other outstanding balance owed by or to the customer. Please allow 4 to 6 weeks for delivery. Offer available while quantities last.

Your Privacy—Your information is being collected by Harlequin Enterprises ULC, operating as Harlequin Reader Service. For a complete summary of the information we collect, how we use this information and to whom it is disclosed, please visit our privacy notice located at corporate.harlequin.com/privacy-notice. From time to time we may also exchange your personal information with reputable third parties. If you wish to opt out of this sharing of your personal information, please visit readerservice.com/consumerschoice or call 1-800-873-8635. **Notice to California Residents**—Under California law, you have specific rights to control and access your data. For more information on these rights and how to exercise them, visit corporate.harlequin.com/california-privacy.

HW21R2

HARLEQUIN SELECTS COLLECTION

19 FREE BOOKS IN ALL!

From Robyn Carr to RaeAnne Thayne to Linda Lael Miller and Sherryl Woods we promise (actually, GUARANTEE!) each author in the Harlequin Selects collection has seen their name on the *New York Times* or *USA TODAY* bestseller lists!

YES! Please send me the **Harlequin Selects Collection**. This collection begins with 3 FREE books and 2 FREE gifts in the first shipment. Along with my 3 free books, I'll also get 4 more books from the Harlequin Selects Collection, which I may either return and owe nothing or keep for the low price of $24.14 U.S./$28.82 CAN. each plus $2.99 U.S./$7.49 CAN. for shipping and handling per shipment*. If I decide to continue, I will get 6 or 7 more books (about once a month for 7 months) but will only need to pay for 4. That means 2 or 3 books in every shipment will be FREE! If I decide to keep the entire collection, I'll have paid for only 32 books because 19 were FREE! I understand that accepting the 3 free books and gifts places me under no obligation to buy anything. I can always return a shipment and cancel at any time. My free books and gifts are mine to keep no matter what I decide.

☐ 262 HCN 5576   ☐ 462 HCN 5576

Name (please print)

Address   Apt. #

City   State/Province   Zip/Postal Code

Mail to the Harlequin Reader Service:
IN U.S.A.: P.O. Box 1341, Buffalo, NY 14240-8531
IN CANADA: P.O. Box 603, Fort Erie, Ontario L2A 5X3

*Terms and prices subject to change without notice. Prices do not include sales taxes, which will be charged (if applicable) based on your state or country of residence. Canadian residents will be charged applicable taxes. Offer not valid in Quebec. All orders subject to approval. Credit or debit balances in a customer's account(s) may be offset by any other outstanding balance owed by or to the customer. Please allow 3 to 4 weeks for delivery. Offer available while quantities last. © 2020 Harlequin Enterprises ULC. ® and ™ are trademarks owned by Harlequin Enterprises ULC.

Your Privacy—Your information is being collected by Harlequin Enterprises ULC, operating as Harlequin Reader Service. To see how we collect and use this information visit https://corporate.harlequin.com/privacy-notice. From time to time we may also exchange your personal information with reputable third parties. If you wish to opt out of this sharing of your personal information, please visit www.readerservice.com/consumerchoice or call 1-800-873-8635. Notice to California Residents—Under California law, you have specific rights to control and access your data. For more information visit https://corporate.harlequin.com/california-privacy.

50BOOKHS22R